Books by Joy Reed

<u>Seraphina Fox Mysteries</u>

The Ghost in the Machine
Poison in Jest
All Hallows' Eve
Night Music
The Hanged Man

Published by Unconsidered Trifle Publications

Published by Zebra Books

The Ghost in
the Machine

The Ghost in the Machine

Being the First Volume of the

Memoirs

of

Madame Seraphina Fox,

Spiritualist,

Describing Her Worldly and Otherworldly

Experiences

Edited by Joy Reed, M.A., B.Sci.

ISBN: 0692768610
ISBN 13: 9780692768617

Dedicated to the
Guild of Extraordinary Gentlewomen

CHAPTER 1

"Is there a disembodied spirit in the room?"

The candle, enclosed in a hanging Moroccan lamp, cast splinters of light across the table. It left the rest of the room in shadow: shadow that seemed to shift and sway with the flickering light. The clients glanced around nervously. It was easy to imagine a ghostly presence lurking just beyond reach of the candle's feeble illumination.

"Is there a disembodied spirit in the room?" I made my voice a singsong chant. Mrs. Gilbert, across the table from me, cast another nervous look around the room, then fixed her eyes on the box in front of us. Her husband, Colonel Gilbert, was staring at the box also. His left hand, clasping my right, felt clammy and cold, and he had unconsciously tightened his grip until my rings pressed painfully into my fingers.

Glancing at the gentleman on my left, I was pleased to see he was no longer wearing the cynical smile that had been hovering on his lips all evening. This was Mr. Jonathan Waggoner, Mrs. Gilbert's brother. He was an avowed skeptic of Spiritualistic Phenomena, but he did not look skeptical now. He was leaning forward tensely, his eyes fixed on the box. His hand in mine was perfectly motionless. Since he had been taking advantage of the darkened room to let his fingers give mine a series of little insinuating squeezes and caresses ever since we had seated ourselves around the table, this made a pleasant change.

"*Is* there a disembodied spirit in the room?" I let a faint note of drama creep into my voice at this third inquiry. And in reply, a bell-like chime sounded within the box.

Mrs. Gilbert gave a stifled cry. The two men jumped slightly, causing their chairs to rattle on the floor. All three of them leaned forward in unison, their eyes riveted on the box in front of us.

It was a wooden box about two feet in length and half as wide, its edges bound and studded in brass like a steamer trunk. On the top surface was a large dial with the alphabet inscribed around its circumference. As the three of them watched with bated breath, the dial began to turn.

"W," breathed Mrs. Gilbert, as the dial came to rest with its indicator pointing to that letter. "W . . . oh, Willie, is it you?"

The bell rang again.

Mrs. Gilbert began to cry. She always cried during our séances with Willie—and this despite the fact that he never failed to assure her of his perfect happiness on the Other Side. It's the kind of thing people expect from their Dear Departed Ones, be they ever such blackened sinners during their time here on Earth.

Happily, there was no reason to think Willie a sinner of this sort. My private researches showed him to have been an amiable young gentleman who had lived a comparatively blameless existence, at least up until the evening he had unwisely drunk too much and entered into a brawl with a professional prize-fighter. But his sister wanted assurances that he was at peace now and bore her no ill will for those little differences that arise even in the most loving families. I was happy to give them to her, even at the cost of a dull evening's work. It's all part of the service I provide for my clients.

They pay handsomely for that service. Not for me the public séance with audience admitted at a shilling a head—not for me the exhibition hall, the cabinet, the bound hands and feet, and the floating trumpets and tambourines—not for me, divining the contents of sealed envelopes in some vulgar sideshow, cheek by jowl with the bearded lady and tattooed man. At least, not anymore. At one time or another I have, admittedly, rung all these changes on the Spiritualistic theme and more besides, but I am beyond all that now. This is, after all, the age of mechanism, of steam, and of scientific advancement. And I have the honour of being London's first truly Scientific Medium, communicating with the Dead via my patented device, the Electrical Spiritograph.

My name is Seraphina Fox.

Or if I am to be perfectly honest with you, Dear Reader, my name is *not* Seraphina Fox—but that is the name by which my clients know me, and the only name I propose to give in this memoir. If I do not reveal my real name, however, rest assured that there will be very few other points on which I am not willing to treat you, the Reader, with the most perfect frankness.

I found it convenient to take the name Seraphina Fox, firstly, because, my real name is far less euphonious—indeed, my parents showed a sad want of imagination at my christening—and secondly, because in common with most other Spiritualistic Mediums I had undergone one or two unpleasant exposures in the past that had slightly tainted the name under which I operated before.

I have been using the name Seraphina Fox for nearly a decade now. You will recognize what a suitable name it is for someone in my line of work: Seraphina suggesting the spiritual, angelic, and other-worldly; and Fox, of course, bringing to mind the famous Fox sisters, pioneers of the Spiritualistic movement. Often people ask if I am related to them, and I always smile and murmur modestly that I believe there is some slight relation. I do not consider this a lie, Dear Reader. According to the Holy Bible, we are all related by way of Adam and Eve—or if you choose rather to believe Mr. Darwin, then it seems reasonable to suppose we are all descended from the same strain of monkey.

But I digress. Here I am talking about monkeys, when I was meaning to speak of Foxes. As I say, I took the name Fox for professional reasons, but it is suitable in a personal sense as well. Not only does my hair happen to be a foxy color between blonde and red (now, alas, showing a few threads of grey), but foxes are clever creatures, known to live on their wits—qualities any successful Medium must possess.

As for those disagreeable people who suggest "Fox" in my case should be spelled "Faux"—that is to say, false or wrong in the French language—I will only point out that my spiritual readings have given general satisfaction. Indeed, I have been so successful that I can afford to turn away many of my would-be clients, selecting only those who most appeal to me.

This is an important point, Dear Reader. Any Spiritualist will tell you that client selection is one of the keys to success in this business. Heaven knows I made enough mistakes early in my career. There was the time that I allowed a frail elderly lady to tie me to my chair, back in the days when I went in for table turning. Unbeknownst to me, she was a rival Medium jealous of my success, and she bound me so securely that I couldn't lift a finger (there was a sad lack of Spiritual phenomena at *that* séance!). Or the time a young gentleman of the press caught me in a rugby tackle as I was flitting about the room banging a tambourine—at a time when I was supposed to be securely tied up inside a cabinet.

Well, let us draw a veil over those painful incidents and others like them. I am older and wiser now. When I came to London ten years ago, I came with the firm intention of reinventing myself, and of profiting from the mistakes I had made before. I now give only small private séances for persons of good family. This has been a winning formula in every way. Now and then I might stretch a point to sit for those who have enough wealth to atone for inferior birth, but those with neither birth nor wealth to recommend them find me regretfully unable to oblige. I also make a point only to accept clients whose backgrounds I have investigated thoroughly. In this way I can exclude the merely curious, the scoffers, the skeptics, and the Radical Press (rude unbelievers to a man, I have found through bitter experience).

Of course, to attract a first-class clientele, it is necessary to have a first-class establishment. My Temple of Spiritualism is in Wimpole Street, a location not grand in itself, but rubbing shoulders with more wealthy districts. My rooms, though not large, are tastefully and imaginatively furnished.

I take care that my personal appearance also fits the image I am trying to project. Although I am no longer in my first youth—or even my second, if it comes to that—I have passed so much of my life in darkened rooms that I have kept my complexion remarkably well. By candlelight, I can still appear handsome enough that men like Mr. Waggoner wish to fondle my hand—and possibly other parts of me as well. That is as it should be. A handsome appearance is a great help to a Spiritualistic Medium.

I still possess a sheaf of yellowing newspaper clippings from the days when I performed in public, describing me as "the lovely Miss So-and-So," and even on occasion "the *beautiful* Miss So-and-So." Between you and me, Dear Reader, my beauty was as much illusion as any of my materializations. I am not and never have been beautiful. This is not to say that my natural appearance would scare the horses in the street, only that I have never hesitated to use cosmetic aids to enhance it.

This, too, is as it should be. Our own dear Queen may condemn paint, powder, false hair, and so forth as vulgar and improper, and you will often hear gentlemen declare all artificial aids to attraction despicable. But take a woman in her natural state, put her side by side with one sporting a padded bosom, a tight-laced corset, a luxuriant crop of false curls, and an artfully enhanced complexion, and see if those same gentlemen do not prefer the latter. This, Dear Reader, is Human Nature: most people are drawn to beautiful illusion over ordinary reality. And this, in a nutshell, is nine-tenths of the appeal of Spiritualism.

Still, if the public is steady in preferring a diet of illusion, it can be fickle in the sort it prefers. There are fashions in illusion, as in all else. In Spiritualism, the first fashion, introduced by the Fox sisters, was rapping on tables—and so we all rapped away for dear life. Then came the fashion for full-figure materializations and cabinets. For a time, there was a fashion for Red Indian spirit controls, and so we all made our spiritual pronouncements in guttural broken English, punctuated with "ughs" and references to the Happy Hunting Grounds.

I followed all these fashions faithfully when I was younger. But when I reached my—let us say my *middle* years—it occurred to me there might be an advantage in setting fashion rather than merely following it. The public is more sophisticated now. Scientific advances have opened up new vistas of possibility. Steam has been harnessed to power locomotives, watercraft, and even airships, while the telegraph conveys messages not merely across continents, but across oceans—a thing hardly less wonderful than speaking to the dead, when you consider it.

This, then, was the inspiration for my Electrical Spiritograph: a telegraph to communicate with the Other Side. I will admit there is not much resemblance to a real telegraph in my device. But the name gives an idea of its purpose that people can readily understand. Since very few of them have any idea how a telegraph works, or indeed any comprehension of electrical principles, my invention has caught the imagination of many who would have otherwise sneered at the idea of Spirit Communication.

There are some original aspects to my design that I am very proud of. My machine has both a device to answer simple yes/no queries—the bell—and an alphabetical clock-face to spell out more involved answers. To anyone who has ever sat through a séance where words had to be laboriously spelled out by reading through the alphabet, the advantage of my system is obvious.

There are other reasons I chose this combination approach. A good séance involves all the senses, or at least as many as can practically be included. So my clients and I hold hands around the table—involving touch—the bell chimes for sound, the alphabet wheel turns for sight—and I like to incorporate scent, too, where possible, as will appear later.

Nor is this all. There is another, more practical reason my Spirits communicate using both a bell and alphabet wheel. A sensible Medium will always have more than one string to her bow! Devices are not always reliable, and if my wheel ceases to turn—as has happened once or twice in the past ten years—we can still communicate using the bell in the old-fashioned way.

Perhaps you will ask now how the device really works. How do the Spirits make the bell ring and the wheel turn? To my clients, I talk a lot of nonsense about Spirit Energy: electric waves emanating from Spirit Sources, which can be converted (through my mediation) into more palpable forms of energy powerful enough to activate a sensitive device like my Spiritograph.[1] But because there are no secrets between you and me, Dear Reader, I will reveal that both bell and wheel are battery-powered rather than spirit-powered, and

---

1 In positing that energy is not destroyed but only transmuted to another form after death, Madame Fox ingeniously draws upon the conclusions of her scientific contemporaries regarding the Law of Conservation of Energy and the First Law of Thermodynamics.—*Ed.*

all that is needed to make them work is to operate a simple switch—two sets of switches, in fact.

The Spiritograph is bolted to the table on which it sets. This is a heavy wooden table with four apparently solid legs and a central pedestal base, studded at intervals with brass studs. It is the most natural thing in the world to rest one's feet on that base during a séance. And if you were to do so, Dear Reader, nothing would happen—but I always wear slippers during my sittings: Turkish slippers beaded and trimmed in silver. Beneath their upturned toes is what appears to be silver brocade, but is, in fact, a surface of pure silver metal, an excellent conductor of electricity. By pressing the toe of my slipper against a particular pair of the metal studs on the pedestal base, the connection is completed. Metal rods running up through the table legs take the power to the box—and the end result is that the bell rings (in the case of the left slipper) or the wheel turns (in the case of the right).

You may be thinking it takes considerable dexterity to operate such a device with one's feet. The wheel is indeed a bit challenging—I geared it to rotate slowly, but it still took a bit of practice to learn how to make it stop on the letter I wanted. Even now I sometimes miss and have to go around a second time. But compared to the difficulty of, say, putting a pencil between one's toes and scrawling words in Spirit Writing on a slate beneath the table, it is child's play.

Only a very slight motion of the foot is needed to operate these switches, much less than that occasioned by rapping, or by the aforementioned Spirit Writing. Still, having been caught out in those pastimes once or twice by spoilsports who looked beneath the table to see what my nether limbs were doing while I sat entranced above, I put another set of switches on the box that I can operate with my hands.

If for any reason I cannot use my foot switches, I simply wait until my clients begin to grow impatient about the lack of phenomena. I then suggest that a more powerful stimulus might be provided by actually laying our hands on the box. On the side of the box that faces me (I always face the same side of it), on the surface just where my thumbs naturally rest, are two sets of brass studs that can be connected the same way as my foot switches. I wear special rings on my thumbs for the purpose. This is much less satisfactory than the foot switches, however. Even after coating the inside of the rings with India-rubber, I still get an occasional nasty shock. This I endure as a necessary cost of doing business.

You can see that I have taken considerable precautions against discovery, Dear Reader. And indeed, I feel confident that my invention would defy almost any scrutiny. To examine the contents of the box, one must unbolt it from the table and disassemble it completely. This would not only prevent it from working, but obscure the way it worked in the first place. Just to be on the safe side, however, the same craftsman who built my table (a useful man who has been years in the trade, building self-rapping devices, movable tables, and the like) made me a second table, identical in appearance to the other, but lacking the metal rods in the legs and the wiring in the base. The box that sits on top of it looks exactly like the other, but would defy the greatest genius on earth to understand its workings! Thus far I have never had to submit it for expert examination, but it stands ready for use if the occasion should ever arise.

As I bade Colonel Gilbert, Mrs. Gilbert, and Mr. Waggoner farewell that evening, I was congratulating myself that tonight would not be the night. I had admitted Mr. Waggoner only reluctantly, knowing him to be a skeptic about Spiritualistic matters. If his sister had not been such a good client of mine, and if she had not made such a point of allowing him to take part ("So that he, too, can speak with our poor dear Willie"), I would never have allowed it.

And if Mr. Waggoner had shown himself half as skeptical in the Spirit Parlour as he had beforehand, his scoffing would have had such a dampening effect on the Spirit Energy that Willie simply would have failed to appear. As is often the case, however, Mr. Waggoner was much less confident and condescending when brought face to face with the Great Unknown.

It is true that he did not speak to Willie as much as his sister did. But he did address one or two questions and seemed genuinely affected by the replies. Once I even saw him blinking tears from his eyes when Willie recounted, via the wheel, a childhood experience they had shared. And though he had given my hand a final squeeze when he took leave of me, it had been a squeeze more grateful than lascivious. It was satisfying to have made a convert out of him, and I was smiling as I threw a dust-cover over the Spiritograph and left the Spirit Parlour, shutting the door behind me.

Susan was waiting in the corridor. Susan is my housekeeper, although to call her that does not convey the half of what she does for me. She has a deceptively quiet, mannerly, and respectable appearance. She opens the door to my clients, takes their coats and hats, and announces their names. And yet I doubt one of them ever gives her a second glance, or realizes that she is at least as intelligent as they are—or as intelligent as I am, if it comes to that.

I fixed her with an accusing eye. "I did not," I said, "feel a Cold Breath touch my face when I first inquired if there were a disembodied spirit in the room."

"The soup wanted stirring," said Susan, sounding not a whit apologetic. "You were such an age getting started that I thought I'd time to slip out for just a minute. But at least I was there to waft 'the breeze freighted with blossom, softly sighing forth from the Summerland.'"

"Yes, and that jasmine is very good quality scent. It's much better than the last stuff the apothecary foisted on us. I vote we keep buying that sort."

Susan agreed that we ought. "There weren't any letters in any of their coat-pockets," she went on. "But Felicity sent a message. She says there's a letter come for Lady Amelia Teague from her son in India. The butler's setting it aside for us as usual, and she'll bring it around tomorrow. Oh, and the soup's ready. Do you want some?"

"Yes, I'm famished. Just let me take off this damnable corset first, so I can enjoy it."

CHAPTER 2

After removing not only the corset, but the veiled headdress, the somber jet-trimmed gown, all ten of the rings, about a pound of false hair, and the artistic shadows painted around my eyes (to make them look haunted and soulful), I threw on my dressing gown and went down to supper. The soup was excellent, and Susan had made an apple tart to go with it.

"Looked like your sitting went well tonight," she commented as we ate.

"Yes, getting our hands on those journals was a great stroke of luck," I said. "Not enough people keep a journal nowadays."

Susan nodded in sad agreement. This is an aspect of the Spiritualism business that you may not realize, Dear Reader. An elite Medium like me employs people whose job it is to stay apprised of sudden, tragic deaths. On hearing of such a death, my agents rush around to the late victim's residence, ostensibly to condole, but really hoping to glean something that might be useful to us: letters, trinkets, or best of all, a diary or journal.

The late Willie Waggoner had been a gold mine in this respect. He lived in lodgings, meaning that a small bribe to his landlady secured us access to his rooms before his family even thought of collecting his things. And he had not only kept a detailed journal, but had done so since childhood. I had ploughed through all eight volumes of it now and felt I knew him better than his own dear mother.

You will say it was heartless of me to keep such priceless personal relics from his family, Reader—worse yet, to use them to extort money from that family. And you may be right, but in my defence let me say that there were passages in those journals that would have disturbed his mother and sister a good deal more than they disturbed me, an experienced judge of Human Nature (and Male Human Nature in particular). Those passages I kindly suppressed. Would you want your nearest and dearest reading about your fumbling attempts to lose your virginity to a series of serving maids and shop-girls? If Willie really could talk, I am sure he would thank me for editing him into a more exalted being.

"The mention of the kite on the church tower turned the trick," I said reminiscently. "If it had just been Mrs. Gilbert, it would have been wasted. She didn't seem to recall the incident at all. But Mr. Waggoner remembered it right away."

"I'll bet you were glad to do something besides just reassuring Mrs. Gilbert that Willie's well and happy," said Susan. "It seems a shame, when we've got so much better material."

I agreed and poured another cup of tea. "Speaking of better material, I'm glad to hear Lady Amelia has got another letter from India. I've been putting her off for a week now, hoping to have some fresh news about her son. Felicity is bringing it tomorrow, you say?"

"Yes, and the butler told her he's found some old letters in a trunk in the attic that might be of use."

This, too, may require some explanation, Reader. Although most of my communications involve Spirits of the Dead, I do sometimes get news of Living Souls through Spirit Sources—especially those Living Souls who live at a goodly distance from London and are faithful correspondents of my regular clientele. You must not be thinking I do anything as illegal as steal people's letters, which would be a serious and actionable offense against the Royal Mail. No, indeed: I simply pay their servants to set aside any suitable letters, so that I may bring them to my Temple, inspect their contents, and note down anything useful they may contain. Then, at the next séance, I announce that so-and-so is expecting a child, or that such-and-such has received a promotion in rank—wait a few days—then finally allow the letter to make its way to its destination, so its recipient may be impressed with the accuracy of my Spirit Sources.

I am told there are honourable servants who refuse to take part in this kind of deception. But I have found most not only willing but eager to help. Not merely for the money, you understand, but as a means of getting back at their employers. Most of these great people pay their domestic staff so poorly and treat them so badly that they are ripe for any mischief. It's a lesson I have taken to heart: my Susan gets extremely generous wages, and the most democratic of treatment.

"Perhaps young Mr. Teague is coming home for another visit," I said. "I can murmur about seeing him on the deck of a ship, riding the waves of the Briny Deep. And you can invoke Sea Breezes and Salt Air." Smell is, after all, the most evocative of the senses, Dear Reader. I have seen a grown man burst into tears when we introduced the scent of lavender, such as his mother used to wear, into my parlour.

For sea breezes, we had an old fishing net that, dampened in a bucket, could be waved back and forth to produce a wonderfully authentic ocean smell. It was a sorrow to me that, thus far, we had enjoyed very few chances to use it: only a single sitting for a deceased admiral, along with a few overseas voyages like Mr. Teague's. Possibly persons connected with the Navy are naturally skeptical about Spiritual matters.

Susan agreed that it would be satisfying to get some more good out of our fishing net, should Lady Amelia's letter contain any suitably nautical reference. "And that reminds me," she added. "There's also a note come for you from Lady Haverhill. She's wanting you to sit for some friends of hers."

These are always words to make me tremble, Dear Reader. My qualms had nothing to do with Lady Haverhill herself. She was one of my favourite clients, a high-spirited old lady who paid me generously each week to call up her late husband so she could keep him up-to-date with the happenings in her life. These séances were the most enjoyable of sittings. I hardly had to do a thing, just ring the bell now and then, or put in a brief word on the wheel. Lady Haverhill preferred to do most of the talking herself, as I learned at our very first séance. When I started spelling out the usual reassuring message about the delights of the Summerland, she had said tartly, "Quit maundering on about flowers, Haverhill, and hear what Ernestine's daughter has done."

I would stretch all possible points for Lady Haverhill. But in fact I already had enough clients without taking on any more. And new clients always posed a potential problem. "I must at least see them, I suppose," I said. "When do they wish to call?"

Susan handed me the note. I read it, and my feeling of misgiving increased. *"My dear Madame Fox, I hope you can help my friends, the Langleys,"* Lady Haverhill wrote. *"Their daughter disappeared a few years ago, and Sophronia Langley's fretted herself to a shadow, wondering what's become of the girl. If convenient, they will call on you tomorrow to make arrangements for a sitting."*

"It's about a missing girl," I told Susan. "Damn it, I *hate* missing people. Dead ones, now—you know where you are with dead ones. If you put words in their mouths, you don't have to worry about them showing up a few months later to contradict you."

Susan consoled me as best she could, but we both knew I would have to at least see the Langleys. "I will write them and put them off a few days, however," I decided. "I'll need to look into the situation and see just what Lady Haverhill has gotten me into."

⸎

I did look into the situation, and the result only increased my misgivings. Mr. and Mrs. Charles Langley were of the Nabob class, Mr. Langley having made a fortune in India like so many other English gentlemen. Their daughter and only child, Elizabeth, had been born in India, but Mr. Langley had sold out of his Indian business a few years after her birth. The family had returned to England, where they had settled not far from London. They lived in a quiet but very comfortable style and were moderately active in their local society.

About three years ago, they had announced an engagement between their daughter and Mr. Giles Roland, a local gentleman of good family. But soon after the engagement was announced, their daughter had apparently vanished into thin air. No one, at any rate, had ever found a trace of her.

At first, in an effort to keep the matter quiet, her parents had hired a well-known firm of private investigators. When they had returned no result, the Langleys had abandoned all effort to keep the matter quiet and blazoned it abroad, calling in the police, inserting pathetic advertisements in all the newspapers begging their daughter to contact them, and offering a generous reward for any information about her whereabouts.

I began my researches, as I usually do, by going through back issues of newspapers. I keep a considerable number of these at the Temple, in the spare room that serves as my personal library as well as housing the dummy Spiritograph. The first newspaper references appeared about the time the police had gotten involved, which was some six months after Miss Langley's actual disappearance. Those first notices were vague but optimistic:

The police are investigating the disappearance of Miss Elizabeth Langley, a young lady of eighteen years of age, who vanished under mysterious circumstances in August of last year.

Miss Langley is the daughter of Mr. and Mrs. Charles Langley, of The Arbours, Hampstead. A young lady of sprightly charm and great personal beauty, she had lately become engaged to Mr. Giles Roland, also of Hampstead. The wedding date had been set, and all parties looking forward to the happy union of the nuptial pair, when matters were thrown into confusion by the sudden and untimely disappearance of the bride-elect.

It was supposed at first that Miss Langley might have suffered some accident, or otherwise been placed in circumstances where she was unable to communicate with her family. Accordingly, the matter was investigated by Mr. Herman Price of Price Investigations, but without returning any conclusive result.

Now that the matter is in the hands of the police, we may hope for a swift resolution of this mysterious affair, which has been such a source of pain and perplexity to Miss Langley's family and friends. The investigation is being conducted by Mr. Thomas Harper, one of Scotland Yard's ablest detective inspectors, whom readers may remember from the recent successful investigation of the Cheltenham jewel theft.

We have learned from Mr. Harper that the police have at present no reason to suspect foul play. It is conjectured that Miss Langley

may have voluntarily left her home with some person or persons un-
known. Early on, suspicions attached to a local gentleman, a former
admirer of Miss Langley, but Mr. Harper says now that those sus-
picions appear to be unfounded and that another clue has recently
been discovered, which appears to furnish a much more likely field
for investigation.

We have no doubt that the police are prosecuting the case with their
usual energy, and that it will not be long before a full and satisfac-
tory explanation of this most perplexing mystery will be laid before
the reading public as well as Miss Langley's anxious family and
friends.

From this optimistic beginning, the newspaper notices soon dwindled into brief and infrequent articles stating merely that the investigation was ongoing. The clue that had promised so much had
apparently delivered nothing, or at least nothing worth mentioning. Equally unproductive had been the sad little advertisement the
Langleys had addressed to their daughter via the agony columns of
seemingly every newspaper in Britain:

Dearest Elizabeth: please communicate through these columns or by
letter. Mama and Papa are anxious to hear from you. A word from
you will set our minds at rest.

I marveled briefly at that reference to "Mama and Papa." Directed
publicly toward a young lady of eighteen on the verge of marriage,
it seemed an infantile—indeed, almost insulting—address. I reminded myself, however, that the Langleys presumably knew what
they were about, and that such terms might be quite usual in their
household. Still, I amused myself by thinking that it might furnish

a motive for Miss Langley's disappearance that the police had not yet considered.

In any case, months had gone by, and the advertisement had produced no result. The police likewise had been graveled for want of material. Just when the matter appeared likely to die out entirely, a fresh infusion of interest was provided by the publication of the following notice:

REWARD: 1000£
Payable for any information leading to the whereabouts of Miss Elizabeth Langley, who went missing on or about August 16 of last year. Age eighteen years; fair hair and complexion, blue eyes, slender build, about five feet three inches in height. Thought to have been wearing a blouse jacket and pleated skirt of blue flower-patterned cambric, white collar and cuffs, patent leather shoes.

If the Police had been wanting clues before, they now had them in abundance. Under the stimulus of the reward money, seemingly half the population of England—as well as quite a few people in Scotland, Wales, and Cornwall—believed they had caught a glimpse of the elusive Miss Langley. She had been seen riding a bicycle along a country lane near Crooksbury Hill. She was spotted taking a medicinal bath at the Harrogate Hydropathic Hotel. A weeping girl answering to her description had been glimpsed boarding the Continental Express in company with a bearded man of sinister aspect.

These sightings, together with the advertisement that prompted them, stimulated a fresh wave of newspaper interest. One of the more sensational papers had no hesitation writing down Miss Langley's disappearance to White Slavery. For a period of weeks, it published a series of titillating articles, rather short on facts but very long on lurid speculation, interspersed with appeals to Parliament to investigate this terrible threat to English young womanhood. What Miss Langley's parents felt about finding themselves at the centre of such a storm, I could only imagine.

With painstaking perseverance, the police had followed up all possible leads. Each and every one of the women thought to be Miss Langley had been traced, interviewed, and found to be someone else entirely. Indeed, in a surprising number of cases, the woman in question proved not only *not* to be Miss Langley, but also proved to be not young, not blonde, not blue-eyed, not slender—in short, was proved in no way to resemble the missing bride-to-be.

You may be surprised at this, Dear Reader, but I was not. I have seen the same phenomenon many times in the course of my career. Perhaps most striking were those occasions a decade or two ago, when I went in for full-figure materializations. After I was tied hand and foot and placed within a wooden cabinet (oftentimes fortified with a locked and barred door), a ghostly figure would appear and flit about the darkened room, shaking a tambourine, tapping people playfully on their shoulders, and going through the rest of the Spiritualistic repertoire then in vogue. I need hardly say that the figure was my own self, freed from bonds that were more substantial in appearance than in fact.

Seeing that this was the case, you would naturally suppose that the figure would be described as looking very much as I do. But you would be wrong, Dear Reader! The people attending my séances regularly described my ghostly figure as resembling a small child—a tall man—a Puck-like figure of indeterminate sex—a skeletal spectre—almost anything besides the woman they had seen tied up and placed inside the cabinet. Through the years, I have come to realize that the illusions I create are only a starting point, as it were. The more spectacular illusions take place inside the minds of my clients.

Clearly a similar process had hampered the search for Miss Langley. I could not wonder at it. When you consider that the audience attending my séances came *expecting* to see Spirits, yet could not describe them accurately afterwards, you can see that casual observers might not be able to accurately describe a woman they glimpsed only in passing. It was perfectly natural, but rather depressing, to see the way clue after clue had petered away to nothing, leaving the case as much a mystery as it had been in the beginning.

Just reading these printed accounts was enough to put me off the idea of sitting for the Langleys. But because I am a conscientious woman in my way, I decided to take my researches one step further and actually speak to some of the people who had been involved in the investigation. *Not* the police, you may be sure: I make it a firm rule to avoid all interactions with the police. Instead, I made an appointment with Mr. Herman Price, the detective agent who had undertaken the first investigation. I represented myself as an agent from another firm who was considering looking into the matter.

Dressing myself in a tailor-made skirt and jacket and a mannish bowler hat, and adorning my countenance with a businesslike pair of spectacles, I hailed a cab and was driven to the office of Price Investigations in Leadenhall Street. After expressing his amusement at the idea of a lady investigator, Mr. Price summed up his opinion of the Langley case by advising me to have nothing to do with it.

"It looked like a simple matter at the outset," he said with a shake of his head. "I figured the gel had agreed to marry Roland, gotten cold feet, and run off with some other fellow instead. Nothing too unlikely in that. Roland's a good-looking lad, but a bit on the bloodless side—not at all what you'd call the answer to a maiden's prayer. What's more, there *was* another fellow who was hankering after her. It was common knowledge there in the neighbourhood where they lived. A Mr. Stern, son of a local squire. Apparently he'd actually gone so far as to make an offer for her and been turned down flat by her parents."

"That sounds suggestive," I said.

"Aye, but there was nothing in it," said Mr. Price sadly. "Because if she'd run off with Stern, he would have disappeared, too—and he hadn't. He's still there, mooning about and telling anyone who'll listen how much he loved her, and how if he'd been as rich as Roland, he would have been accepted instead. He told me so himself."

That sounded suggestive to me, too, Dear Reader, but in a more sinister way. People like to quote that old adage about Hell having no fury like a woman scorned, but if you read the newspapers as closely as I do, you will have noted many accounts of scorned men taking a violent revenge on the women who rejected them. Many a wronged woman will make violent threats in a like situation, of course, but few ever really act on their fury.

In any case, it sounded exactly the kind of mess I didn't want to touch, and I told Susan so when I got back to the Temple. "I'll see the Langleys, but I'll make it clear I can't do anything. Much as I hate to disoblige Lady Haverhill, I can't be expected to succeed where the police, the public, and a firm of private investigators have failed."

CHAPTER 3

In the end, I decided that rather than having the Langleys call upon me (my usual practice with prospective clients), I would call upon them instead. Because I meant to refuse them, I felt I would rather keep them both figuratively and physically at arm's length and not let them anywhere near the Temple of Spiritualism.

The Langleys lived not far out of London, in a village that was now a suburb of the great city. I got there by cab easily enough. It was less than an hour's drive, and a fine day for it, too, with the sun shining as it does all too seldom in England's not-so-sunny clime.

I found the Langleys' residence without difficulty. It was one of the principal houses of the neighbourhood: The Arbours, a handsome red brick building with a three-story central block, spreading wings, and a columned entrance portico. A well-kept drive led from the gates across an open expanse of parkland, rising to where the house sat surrounded by gardens still showing a riot of color despite the approach of autumn. Having asked the driver to wait for me, I got out of the cab, adjusted the veil swathing my head and shoulders, and walked slowly toward the door. I was dreading the interview ahead, but consoled myself with the idea that it would soon be over.

Mrs. Langley had obviously been on the watch for me. "Madame Fox! I am so glad you are here," she said, waving aside her butler and taking me familiarly by the arm as soon as I was admitted to the house.

She kept up a quick, nervous patter of conversation as she led me into a pretty drawing room furnished in shades of muted gold and old rose. "Sit down, please. I'll tell Roberts to bring us some tea. And here is Mr. Langley. We have both been so anxious to meet you."

It did not take much psychic ability to divine that this was a bald-faced lie, in the case of Mr. Langley, at least. Never have I seen reluctance written larger on a human countenance. I thought I saw distaste there, too, or something like it, so I generously refrained from making him shake hands with me. I merely bowed before taking a seat on a pastel armchair that accorded ill with my black dress. Once seated, I pushed the veil back from my face.

Both Langleys recoiled slightly. Even though I was refusing their commission—in fact, partly *because* I was refusing their commission—I had taken care to appear in the full regalia of my profession: the veil, the funereal black-plumed hat, the rings and beads and amulets, the pallid complexion and artful shadows around the eyes. In fact, I had deliberately striven for a theatrical effect. If they rejected me before I rejected them, well and good: I would have done my duty by Lady Haverhill and could abandon the matter with a clear conscience.

Mrs. Langley, however, quickly recovered from her initial shock. Dropping into the chair nearest me, she grasped my hand between hers and began speaking again in her quick, nervous voice. "Lady Haverhill has given us such an amazing account of you and your powers. My dear Madame Fox, if you could possibly help us! We have tried *everything*. It's the uncertainty that is hardest to bear. If we could only be *certain*, even if we were to learn that Elizabeth is—is—is no longer with us. Yes, even if she is dead, I think it would be easier. Not at the outset, of course, but in time."

I said nothing, and she took up her speech again, describing how Lady Haverhill had praised me, how all others had failed, and how desperately she and Mr. Langley wanted help in finding a solution to the mystery poisoning their existence.

I am not a soft-hearted woman, Dear Reader. One cannot afford to be, in my business. But I could not help feeling profoundly sorry for her as she talked on and on, staring at me all the while with a desperate appeal in her eyes. Talk of your haunted eyes! All my efforts with India ink, lamp-black, and grease-pencil fell woefully short to what Sophronia Langley had achieved through three years of maternal suffering. Her eyes were ringed with bruised-looking shadows—natural, not artificial like mine—and they filled with tears as she looked at the portrait that hung above the fireplace.

"That is she," she said. "That is Elizabeth. It was painted only a few months before she disappeared."

I, too, looked at the portrait. Although the newspaper articles had given me a general idea of Miss Langley's appearance, their written descriptions could not convey the same detail as a visual likeness. The portrait depicted a slender fair-haired girl holding an armful of flowers and leaning over a garden gate. There was a great resemblance to her mother in the large, light blue eyes and the fine-boned delicacy of the face.

In fact, looking at the portrait, I thought that Elizabeth Langley looked a little too fine altogether for this rude Earth: more angel than flesh-and-blood woman. There was something in the curve of the mouth and the expression of the painted eyes that hinted at sensitivity and a shrinking from notice. Artists do take liberties with the appearance of their subjects, of course—especially when those subjects are wealthy society people. But sometimes they also succeed in capturing more of their subjects' personality than might appear in a straightforward photograph.

"It's a beautiful portrait," I said. "Your daughter was—is—a beautiful girl."

I cursed myself for my clumsiness as soon as the words were out of my mouth. As I had feared, Mrs. Langley caught at them. "Was? Or is? Can you—do you know? Have you *seen* anything? At one of your sittings?"

"No, no," I said quickly. "Not at all. In fact—" I drew a deep breath, "in fact I am afraid I will not be able to help you, Mrs. Langley."

At these words, Mr. Langley stirred slightly. He had said nothing so far, but simply sat in his chair, watching me with his arms folded across his chest. It was perfectly obvious that he hated the whole business. I did not place over-much emphasis on that fact, however. The husbands of many of my female clients are wont to regard me askance. One cannot altogether blame them if one considers the matter dispassionately. In any case, on this issue, the two of us were in complete accord. Turning to him, I addressed him directly.

"I think you would rather I did not act in this matter, Mr. Langley?"

He frowned. "Why would you think that?" he asked. And then, without giving me opportunity to answer, he added, "Indeed, I would be very glad to know what has become of Elizabeth. I am not disposed to look upon the matter in so desperate a light as my wife, however. Elizabeth was our only child. We took great pleasure in gratifying all her wishes, almost before she could express them. I daresay we spoiled her. And young women today—one hears so many stories of wayward, and willful, and impulsive behaviour."

"You believe she has run away?"

"Elizabeth would never have run away," cried Mrs. Langley. "Not like this—not without sending me word."

"It's the only explanation," said Mr. Langley, ignoring his wife's outburst. "Considering how thoroughly the police and the private detectives we employed looked into the matter, I cannot believe they would not have turned up some sign of her by now if she had met with some unfortunate fate."

"It is my understanding that they turned up no sign of her at all," I pointed out. "That means there is no indication *what* kind of fate she met."

He looked at me for a moment, evidently weighing his words. "True," he said at last. "But I daresay we shall learn it in time."

"It has been more than three years now," cried his wife, who had been listening to this exchange with mounting impatience. "I cannot bear it, Charles. I must know what has happened to her."

"I doubt you will learn it by employing a *Spiritualist*," he said, with cutting scorn. "In any case, Madame Fox has said she cannot act, so there is nothing more to be said."

This was exactly the response I was hoping for, Dear Reader, so I cannot explain why I reacted as I did. It's often said that red-haired people are hot-tempered. I do not put much stock in those kinds of generalizations, and my hair is not as red as all that in any case. But something in Mr. Langley's speech roused me to ire. To speak in that sneering way of my profession was bad enough, but to my mind, the way he spoke to his wife was even worse. I have always disliked men who address their wives in that lordly, dismissive manner. It's one of the reasons I have never married.

So when Mrs. Langley turned to me and said, "But she *will* act for us—I know she will! You cannot be so cruel as not even to try?" I paused as if deliberating and then said, "No, I will try if you insist, ma'am. But you must not expect anything to come of it."

I had plenty of time to regret my words as Mrs. Langley was showering me with thanks and her husband was looking on with cold disapproval. I continued to regret them as I rode home in my cab. As if in sympathy with my mood, the day had clouded over, and the smiling countryside no longer seemed so smiling. I saw glimpses of ruin and decay everywhere I looked: in the turning leaves, the shorn fields, and the fallen-down church tower I glimpsed through the trees as the driver negotiated the turn onto the high road.

When I finally got back to the Temple, I was met by Susan, brimming with cheer and blithely confident that the Langley affair was now closed, docketed, and put away for good. She was incredulous when I told her what I had done.

"What on earth possessed you? I thought you were opposed to the whole idea!"

"I was. I am. I don't know what came over me," I said. Sinking down onto the Sitting Room sofa, I put my head in my hands. "But I am committed now. Anyway," I added, with an attempt at looking on the brighter side, "this way I'll at least get full credit for trying with Lady Haverhill. That is worth a good deal."

"I suppose so," said Susan, eyeing me askance. "But not knowing whether the girl is alive or dead leaves you in a bit of a fix, doesn't it? Won't you have to commit yourself when her parents ask the Spirits what's become of her?"

"No, not necessarily. I have been thinking, and I've decided there will be no Spirit response at all. I have a good enough reputation that I can afford to fail once in a while. Besides, it's good policy. People think it proves you're honest. They reason that if you were fraudulent, you would always get a response."

Susan allowed there was something to this, and I told her that I was to sit for the Langleys the following evening. "Short notice," she said, eyeing me askance once more. "But then, as I suppose as you don't mean the Spirits to respond, there's no need to spend time swotting up on your clients beforehand."

This was true, and I agreed, but it wasn't the whole truth, Dear Reader. In fact, my setting an early date for the séance had been prompted simply by a desire to get the whole business over and done with.

After breakfast the next morning, we began to ready the Spirit Parlour for the evening's sitting. "Since you're not planning to receive any messages, are you going to use the dummy table and machine?" Susan asked.

"No, I see no need for that," I said. "Mr. Langley appears to be a skeptic, but I don't see him making any kind of fuss if I fail. Besides, you never know. I might think of some way for the Spirits to respond that will comfort Mrs. Langley, without definitely saying one way or another whether her daughter is alive." I kept hoping I could think of a way to do this.

You may not believe me, Dear Reader, but I often do bring comfort to my clients. When Death comes, it does not always allow the luxury of a final farewell to one's family and friends. In the case of sudden and unexpected death, especially, survivors are often left with regrets about things said and unsaid, or some real or fancied neglect on their part. I have seen many a man and woman sob wildly in the catharsis of the séance and received many a generous cheque the following day, accompanied by a note overflowing with gratitude.

I couldn't honestly see how I would achieve this in Mrs. Langley's case. But I do get wonderful inspirations sometimes during the course of a sitting. Being under pressure often seems to improve one's performance, I have found.

At any rate, I was glad I did not have to sit down at the table and spell out my own belief about Elizabeth Langley's fate. For in my heart of hearts, I felt certain she was dead. I have seen enough of life to know how often tragedy befalls even the young and beautiful, Dear Reader. And there had been something strongly suggestive of tragedy about that particular young and beautiful face. Or perhaps it was simply that her mother had seemed so sure that if she were alive, she would have communicated somehow. A mother's instinct is not to be sneezed at.

Still, even if Mrs. Langley's instinct were correct, I could not bring myself to deprive her of hope. One of our best and wisest authors has called hope the greatest of all treasures,[2] and though I myself might plump for a comfortable balance at the banker's, there is much in what he says. If the Spiritograph spoke at all, I was determined that its message would be hopeful.

I don't leave these things to chance if it can be avoided. I spent most of that afternoon inventing, then discarding, various vague and hopeful messages. I was still at it when Susan told me a gentleman wished to see me.

"A gentleman?" I repeated. My mind flew at once to Mr. Langley. After the antagonism he had shown yesterday, it would not be surprising if he tried to cancel the séance tonight. "An older gentleman—tall but not stout—light, thinning hair and a rather cold blue eye?"

"No, a young one—dark, and good-looking, too." She handed me a card bearing the name of Mr. Giles Roland.

The name was familiar, and after a moment I placed it. Giles Roland had been Elizabeth Langley's affianced husband. "Oh, dear," I said, looking down at the card. "It only gets worse."

"You want me to refuse him?"

---

2 This statement evinces real spiritualistic ability on the part of Madame Fox. The author she cites, Sir Terry Pratchett, is contemporary to our time, not hers. One infers that despite her generally dismissive attitude about her abilities as a Medium, she did possess true precognitive powers.—*Ed.*

"No, I'd better see him," I decided, my professional instincts taking over. "We might get something out of him. Take his hat and coat, put him in the Sitting Room, and I'll be along directly."

As soon as the corset had been tightened, the black dress and veiled headpiece donned, the rings and lace mittens fitted onto my hands, and the carpet slippers exchanged for black kid boots, I went down to the Sitting Room. "I am Madame Fox," I said, leaving the door ajar behind me and taking care to speak in a clear, loud (but not ungenteelly loud) voice. "You wish to speak to me?"

Mr. Roland had risen politely at my entrance and stood looking at me, twisting his gloves in his hands. I think my appearance surprised him, Dear Reader. It usually does surprise people, but he had one of those faces that is hard to read. "Yes," he said at last, in a voice quite as clear as mine and very precise in its articulation. "I spoke with Mrs. Langley, and I heard about what is being planned for this evening. You don't know who I am, of course, but—"

"I do know who you are," I said, in a thrilling tone that implied I knew all his darkest secrets. I fear it was wasted on him, however. He only nodded, looking dubious. So I bade him sit down, sat down myself, and proceeded to draw out of him as much as I could.

I could see what Mr. Price had meant about his being "bloodless" and "not the answer to a maiden's prayer." At the same time, I thought it slightly unfair. The detective had been a brawny man, broad of shoulder and a good six feet tall. It stood to reason that he would not have admired Giles Roland's type, but it was a type that might appeal to many women.

Mr. Roland was barely of average height and very slim in his build. His dark hair was combed smoothly over his well-shaped head, and his features had the regularity of a Greek statue's. His eyes, like those of his missing fiancée, were wide and blue, and indeed I was struck by a certain resemblance between him and Elizabeth Langley.

Both had that same sensitive cast of countenance, with its suggestion of inward shrinking and reserve.

Reserved or not, Mr. Roland had come here to open his heart to me. "I have never had dealings with this sort of thing," he told me, waving a hand to indicate my Sitting Room with its purple brocade hangings, paintings of mystical subjects, and dimly exotic atmosphere. "I am not sure I believe in Spirit Communication. At the same time, I am willing to think there might be something in it. One hears of so many people who have received messages that cannot be explained in the normal way."

I inclined my head slightly, indicating that he should go on.

"I know how painfully Mrs. Langley has felt her daughter's disappearing in such a way." He looked at me earnestly. "I have felt it, too, Madame Fox. I was engaged to marry Elizabeth Langley, and it was a suitable marriage in every way. Both our families were in favour of the match. We had set the date for the wedding, and I was looking about for a suitable house in the neighbourhood, not too far from the Arbours, where her parents live. She was very attached to her parents."

"I had gathered she and her mother were very close," I said, choosing my words with care. "Was she close to her father as well? I must say I did not get that impression from speaking with him."

Rather to my surprise, Mr. Roland shook his head decidedly. "You must not be misled by Langley's manner. He was very protective of Elizabeth, very attached to her. I often remarked it."

This was disappointing. The fact is, Dear Reader, that ever since making his acquaintance, I had been toying with the idea that Mr. Langley might have had something to do with his own daughter's disappearance. He had seemed so dismissive of the idea that any harm could have come to her, and so insistent that nothing more need be done in the matter. Besides, he had also been rude to *me*. I would have liked very well to cast him as the villain of the piece, but supposed I would have to make allowances for an English gentleman's dislike of the sensational, coupled with a more hopeful temperament than his wife's.

Mr. Roland, meanwhile, had gone on speaking. "I still find it completely inexplicable that Elizabeth should have disappeared as she did. I had thought she was as eager to be married as I was, despite some natural reservations."

These last words caught my attention. "She had reservations about marrying you?"

"Oh, no," he said quickly. "I know she loved me. Indeed, the last time we met, she said over and over how much she loved me. There were tears in her eyes when she said it."

I looked him over with new attention. One soon learns in my business to detect evasion. "But still she had reservations?" I insisted.

"No more than were natural. She was, after all, a gently-bred, innocent girl. Indeed, she was more angel than girl, Madame Fox. I often told her so. And marriage—well, some aspects of marriage would naturally shock a girl like that. Naturally they would." He stopped, a slight flush suffusing his face.

"You thought she might shrink from the *physical* aspects of marriage," I said, in a matter-of-fact voice.

"That's it," he said gratefully. "That's it exactly. I knew she would . . . shrink from those aspects. And so when she told me she couldn't marry me, of course I knew what it was about."

Now he really had my attention. "She told you she couldn't marry you?"

"Yes, but it was only that she was so pure—so innocent. You could see it in her eyes. Beautiful as an angel, with a soul clear as crystal. I wasn't fit to touch even the hem of her skirt, as I often told her."

This kind of talk turns my stomach, Dear Reader. It's quite in order for a man to think well of the woman he loves. And of course he should treat her kindly and with respect—that goes without saying. But this putting a woman on a pedestal and talking as though she were made of moonbeams and angel wings is a bad business. No woman could live up to such an image, and life would hardly be worth living for the woman who could.

I myself had been struck by the angelic quality of Miss Langley's appearance, but I was not fool enough to take it at face value. No one knows better than I how deceptive appearances can be.

"Perhaps you frightened her," I said, meaning to try to convey this as kindly as I could. But of course Mr. Roland misunderstood me.

"No, indeed! You must not think I did more than kiss her," he assured me. "And that in the most respectful way."

This made my stomach churn yet harder. "I don't doubt it," I said. "But are you sure her reservations had to do with that?"

He stared at me, obviously bewildered. "What else could it have been?" he asked. "I know she loved me. She said so often, and she was such a good, pure girl. She would never have lied, and certainly not about that. She had such good Christian principles. Indeed, she was as humble as she was good and beautiful. She told me that *she* wasn't worthy of *me*."

"She told you that?"

"Yes, that was the reason she gave for not marrying me."

"And what do you suppose she meant by it?"

"I didn't suppose she meant anything at all. She was so obviously above me." He looked at me earnestly. "I was certain it was only that she shrank from—you know."

On the whole, I thought he was telling the truth, or at least the truth as he saw it. But he was so obtuse that I couldn't be sure he hadn't overlooked the obvious.

I decided to ask the question directly. "You don't think Miss Langley might have wished to break her engagement with you, in order to marry someone else?"

"Certainly not!" Both his voice and expression were outraged. "She loved me, and I loved her. There was no question of anything of that sort."

"Yet I had heard there was another suitor—another man who wished to marry her."

His brow wrinkled, then cleared. "You are talking about Jim Stern. Yes, he was disposed to admire her, certainly. But there was nothing in it. They were friends as children, nothing more."

"I had heard there was *something* more. Is it not true that Mr. Stern had proposed to marry her and been turned down by her parents?"

It appeared this was news to Mr. Roland. But he soon recovered himself. "It's no wonder if Stern admired her and wanted to marry her. Any man would. But she was engaged to *me*. And she assured me she had never loved anyone as she loved me."

To my mind, this still left the matter wide open, but I doubted I would shake his conviction. "What do you believe happened to her?" I asked instead.

"Some kind of accident," he said promptly. "Perhaps she was injured and lost her memory. One often hears of such things happening."

One mainly heard such things in the more romantic sort of novel, but I refrained from voicing this statement aloud. "It might be," I agreed, humouring him. "But her mother fears it is more serious than that."

He nodded, his expression solemn. "And you really believe you can find out, Madame Fox? That you can . . . speak with Elizabeth in some way?"

Of course I believed nothing of the sort, but I rolled my eyes heavenward and murmured that we might learn something tonight if the Spirit Energy were strong enough. "Would it help if I were there?" he asked. "Of course I am not a true believer, as I told you before. But I find the subject interesting and am willing to keep an open mind."

Deciding I might as well be hanged for a sheep as a lamb, I told him that he could attend the séance if he desired. He wanted to know what preparations he ought to make beforehand. Should he bathe and change into fresh clothing? Truly, that young man had purity on the brain. I told him it might help and couldn't hurt and sent him on his way.

After he was gone, Susan and I talked over what we had learned. "Do you think he had anything to do with Miss Langley's disappearance?" she asked.

"No," I said. "But it's difficult to be sure. He's either a complete ninny or an excellent actor, and either way one can't trust what he says. It sounds as though the poor girl did have some kind of qualms about marrying him, doesn't it? But perhaps that's only what we're meant to think."

All in all, I felt the information I had gained from Mr. Roland had only muddied the waters. I was still uncertain about what Miss Langley's Spirit ought to say that evening. So I reverted to my first plan to say nothing at all. Mr. Roland would be disappointed in his first contact with Spiritualism, but that couldn't be helped.

CHAPTER 4

Afternoon passed; evening fell; and when the appointed hour came, there were four of us gathered around the Electrical Spiritograph. I consider four the ideal number for a séance, but we were hardly an ideal group all the same.

I could not fault Mrs. Langley's attitude, unless it were that she was so aflame with eagerness that it hurt to look at her. But Mr. Roland, as he glanced around the Spirit Parlour with its black velvet draperies, alabaster lamps, and statues of what he would almost certainly have called heathen gods and goddesses, looked as though he were sorry he had come—or perhaps he was merely worrying that it might not be hygienic. Mr. Langley sat scowling at the Spiritograph, his arms folded across his chest in his usual posture of disapproval.

"What are we waiting for?" he asked, his tone conveying clearly that he regarded the whole business as folly, and that the sooner it was over the happier he would be.

"We are almost ready," I told him. "Let me turn down the lamps, and then we will join hands around the table."

He snorted, but I thought there was a shade of uneasiness in his eyes as he watched me move around the room extinguishing the lamps, until the only light came from the single candle in the Moroccan lantern over our heads. When I returned to the table and took his hand in mine, he made no objection. He was sitting on my right and Mr. Roland on my left, with Mrs. Langley across the table from me.

As I sat there in my Spirit Parlour, I could not help feeling depressed. Picture an actress, Dear Reader, letter-perfect in her rôle, and yet forced to go onstage and deliberately flub her lines. That is how I felt. I knew I had the means to astonish and impress my little audience, but I was deliberately refraining from using them.

We sat and sat in the darkened room, the candlelight flickering around us and the Spiritograph silent and motionless in front of us. We sat for over an hour, and I rather expected Mr. Langley to say something about its all being a waste of time, but he seemed content to sit and wait.

I avoided looking at Mrs. Langley. I didn't care to see the hope fading from her eyes. I didn't care to look at Mr. Roland, either, for his prim demeanour was beginning to irritate me. Instead I shut my eyes and focused on the little sounds in the room: the measured breathing of my companions, the faint sizzle of wax from the candle, and now and then a soft stirring that I thought might be Susan in the next room.

Gradually I became aware of something else: not a sound, but a smell. It was a cold, earthy, underground sort of smell. I wondered if Susan had left a window open. There appeared to be a draught coming from somewhere, bringing the smell along with it. It was certainly not one of *my* smells, Dear Reader. My Spirits are all happy Spirits, cavorting freely in the fields of the Summerland, not shut mouldering away in their tombs.

This smelled distinctly like a tomb.

My eyes flew open. Mrs. Langley was staring at me across the table, her eyes dilated with fear. Mr. Langley's hand trembled in mine. Mr. Roland's eyes flashed wildly around the room, betraying a panic his set face did not reveal.

I knew it must be imagination or coincidence: some freak occurrence of perfectly natural origin. It wasn't going to affect my resolve. The Spiritograph was not going to speak that evening. I could feel the other three staring at me, expecting me to do or say something. But I gritted my teeth and kept my mouth shut even as the cold, earthy smell grew stronger and stronger around us.

I had reckoned without Mrs. Langley, however. All at once, she lifted her head and called out her daughter's name. "Elizabeth," she cried. "Elizabeth, is it you?"

And the bell rang.

I must have moved my left foot and closed the circuit by mistake. It was the only explanation. I took both feet off the table pedestal, then put them back on again, realizing I was committed now. I couldn't leave the matter like this. I could hear Mr. Roland's breath coming in little gasps, and feel Mr. Langley's hand trembling like a leaf in mine. Tears were running down Mrs. Langley's face, but there was awe and exultation there, too, as she spoke again.

"Elizabeth," she said, "oh, my darling, why did you leave us? What happened?"

How to answer? My right foot hesitated over the contacts for the wheel. Something indefinite—an apology—an assurance that all was well. That would be my normal response to a question of that sort, though I wasn't sure I could manage the assurance part in the face of that all-too-suggestive earthy smell. But the apology was simple enough. Pressing my right foot down, I began to spell out "Sorry."

"S," breathed Mr. Roland, watching the wheel move.

When I went to spell the "O," however, the wheel stopped short at "I," nor could I make it move again despite a good many surreptitious scufflings with my slipper. "I," said Mr. Roland. He exchanged glances with the Langleys.

The wheel switch was obviously malfunctioning. I removed my feet from the pedestal and opened my mouth to suggest we lay hands on the box. That's when the wheel began to turn again, coming to rest on the letter "N." And there it remained, in spite of anything I could do with either of my feet.

"Sin?" said Mr. Roland with a questioning inflection. And the bell rang again.

I believe I felt more exasperation than anything else, Dear Reader. To use the actress analogy again, I had just been upstaged. "Sin," cried Mrs. Langley. "What sin? Oh, Elizabeth, what do you mean? Where are you?"

We all watched as the wheel clicked slowly around to spell "C-R-Y-P-T." In spite of some very mixed feelings, I could not help being impressed. It was, after all, the first time I had viewed the Spiritograph as a mere spectator.

"Crypt?" said Mrs. Langley doubtfully. "I don't understand." Then her eyes widened. "Crypt!" she cried. "Oh, Charles, do you think . . . the old church? I remember hearing there *was* a crypt, though it was supposed to have fallen in ages ago."

Mr. Langley looked like a man who had seen a ghost—which, come to think of it, was not far from the fact. "It could be," he said in a hoarse voice. Pulling his hand away from mine, he got out his handkerchief and buried his face in it, his shoulders shaking with emotion.

This broke the circle, Dear Reader. I used it as an excuse to get up and relight the lamps. Everyone looked shaken. Indeed, I felt shaken myself.

Mr. Roland kept uttering little ejaculations under his breath: "Upon my word, I hardly—indeed, one hardly knows what to think." Mr. Langley kept his face buried in his handkerchief. Mrs. Langley turned to me at last, her face a mask of tragedy.

"I thank you," she said. "We all thank you. Of course, this must be looked into."

I glumly agreed that it must.

"We will let you know, Madame Fox. For myself, I have no doubt. But we will let you know." Despite her tragic face, there was energy and decision in her manner. It was she who got both men on their feet and moving toward the door.

Outside in the corridor, Susan appeared with their hats and coats. As soon as they were all safely out the door, Susan shut it behind them, then turned to look at me.

"By all that's wonderful," she said, "would you mind telling me what happened in there?"

I put a hand to my aching head. "Make me a cup of tea first," I said. "Or better yet, bring me a glass of brandy." Over-indulgence in Spirits of that sort has ruined the career of many a promising Medium, Dear Reader, as I well knew. I normally limit myself to an occasional glass of wine, but there are times when strong liquor is helpful to dull the edges of reality when it becomes a little too real.

Susan had some brandy, too, while I gave her a full account of the séance. "That smell!" she said. "I smelled it, too. Even in the next room, it was clear as clear. I couldn't think what was happening. And then when the bell rang—"

I shuddered. "Yes. The first time, I thought I had touched the switch by mistake. Perhaps I did."

"But it wasn't you after that? Nor you that spelled the words?"

I shook my head. "I can believe—just barely believe—that 'sin' was an accident. That the wheel might have malfunctioned. For I did spell the 'S.' I was meaning to say something like 'sorry to make you worry—all is well.'"

Susan gave a short laugh. "And instead you end up telling them she's in a crypt somewhere!"

"Yes," I said, wincing a little at this bald statement of fact. Reality still needed a little dulling. I took another sip of brandy. "Mrs. Langley said something about an old church in the neighbourhood, with a crypt that had fallen in. And the others seemed to know what she was talking about and think it possible."

I frowned, for the words had stirred a chord of memory. "An old church . . . good heavens, yes. I remember seeing an old church tower through the trees, that day I drove out to the Arbours. I remember thinking at the time that it looked as though it was falling into ruins. It isn't far from the Arbours, either—not far at all."

"Do you think the girl's really there? And that they'll find her?"

This was a question indeed, Dear Reader. To say "yes" would mean suspending a lifetime of skepticism, built on a solid foundation of experience. "Yes," I said glumly. "I'm very much afraid they will."

"Well, but that wouldn't be so bad, would it? Indeed, it would make you look pretty good. To find her after the police and private detectives had failed—"

"It's not at all the sort of thing that will do me good," I said. "The last thing I want is to be mixed up in a murder investigation. That sort of publicity would have been all very well back in the days when I performed in the music halls, but my clients nowadays won't appreciate it at all."

"So you think it's murder?" asked Susan, round-eyed. "But why? Couldn't it just as well be suicide, or an accident?"

I had to stop and think about this. I felt perfectly sure it was murder, but why? "I suppose it's the mention of sin," I said. "Of course that might apply to suicide, too, but in that case her body would probably have turned up by now, instead of being hidden in some fallen-down church crypt. And she would probably have left a note as well. Most suicides do."

"Perhaps someone destroyed the note, or hid it?" suggested Susan. But she could think of no good reason why anyone would do this, and neither could I.

On the other hand, I had no difficulty at all guessing there would be trouble. It didn't take an Electrical Spiritograph to see that. "If they do find her body, the police are going to come and ask me how I knew where she was," I predicted with gloomy certainty. "It's most unjust. After I've been so successful in avoiding their attention, all these past ten years! But it can't be helped. At any rate, I certainly can't afford to take chances."

I drew a sigh. "Send notes around to my clients and tell them I'm cancelling all my sittings for the next week. Tell them I'm ill. And before we go to bed tonight, we must swap the dummy table for the one in the Spirit Parlour. The last thing we need is for it to start spelling out inconvenient truths while the police are here!"

CHAPTER 5

A couple of days later, my prophecy was fulfilled. Susan came into my bedroom, her face ominous. "There's a policeman downstairs," she said. "He wants to see you. Here's his card."

I surveyed it gloomily. "Detective Inspector Thomas Harper. Yes, of course; he's the one the newspapers said was handling the Langley investigation. Very well, Susan. Put him in the Sitting Room and tell him I'll be down shortly."

It took a little time before I was ready to see the Inspector. I thought it well to moderate my usual appearance. First impressions count for a great deal, and I wanted the Inspector's first impression of me to be one of, above all, respectability.

He stood on my entering the room, a tall lean man of middle years with dark hair and an aquiline profile. He was not precisely handsome, but his face was pleasant enough, with a mouth that looked as though it smiled easily. The general effect would have been reassuring, had it not been mitigated by a pair of uncommonly sharp grey eyes. I could see those eyes taking stock of my black silk dress, my smoothly drawn-back hair, and my (apparently) un-retouched face as he introduced himself.

"I've come about this business of Elizabeth Langley," he said. "And a very bad business it is, too. I suppose you've heard?" He fixed me with a keen grey eye.

I am far too old a hand to be taken in by this kind of thing. "Heard what?" I inquired, gazing back at him innocently.

"Then you did not know that they have found Miss Langley's body?"

I didn't have to act the unhappiness I felt at these words. "No, I did not know. I am sorry indeed to hear it. Poor Mrs. Langley. And Mr. Langley, too, of course," I added conscientiously. I was thinking a little better of that gentleman after seeing the way he had broken down at the séance table.

The Inspector was still regarding me closely. "I had understood it was you who told the Langleys where they might find their daughter."

"In a manner of speaking," I said guardedly.

"The police are naturally interested to learn how you came into possession of that information. I would be much obliged if you would tell me all about it."

There was nothing I felt less like doing, but I bade him sit down and ask me any questions he liked, adding virtuously that of course I was happy to help the police in any way I could.

"Thank you, Miss Fox," he said, taking out a notebook and regarding me again with those bright, inquisitive eyes. "Or should it be Mrs. Fox?"

"Madame Fox, if you please."

"And that is spelled F-O-X?" he asked. Though his voice was sober enough, something in his manner of speaking made me sure he had seen the lampoon that had appeared recently in one of the radical newspapers, referring to me as Madame Faux. Fortunately, few of my clients read that type of newspapers.

I told him yes, it was F-O-X, and kindly offered to write it out for him. He said that wasn't necessary. "Christian name?"

"Seraphina. *That* is spelled—"

"I know how to spell it, thank you, Madame." I felt I had won that round, and his reluctant smile conceded it. "Your age?"

"Thirty-five," I said, promptly and inaccurately. He cocked a skeptical eyebrow, but wrote it down without comment.

"And you are a . . . Spiritualist by trade?"

"Yes, I am," I said, turning my face gently to the light so he could appreciate the truly spiritual cast of my countenance.

"And you claim to have gotten the information about Miss Langley's whereabouts from . . . spirit sources?"

I did not answer immediately, but sat looking at him long enough to make him uncomfortable (I hoped). "I have made no claim at all," I said. "Didn't the Langleys tell you what happened?"

He nodded. "Yes, but I tell you frankly I have a difficult time believing it. In my experience, Madame, most persons in your line of work are—you'll pardon me for saying so—charlatans."

It was my turn to arch a brow. "If you feel that way, I wonder you bother to ask me for information!"

"Well, I'm willing to believe there might be an exception to the rule," he said good-humouredly. "I've been making inquiries about you, and I'm obliged to say that your customers give you a very good character."

I informed him that the preferred term was *clients*. "But I am pleased to hear they give me a good character," I said, casting my eyes down modestly. "One does one's poor best."

"Well, in the vulgar parlance, you seem to have brought home the goods all right, in the Langley affair," he said. "Would you tell me how you did it? I understand you practice some kind of . . . table-turning?"

"Table-turning!" I exclaimed. I did not bother to conceal my outrage, Dear Reader. "Indeed I do not! Table-turning is simply a parlour trick. And quite an outdated one as well," I added sternly.

He looked puzzled, but apologized very properly. "Then what is it you do? Can you show me?"

Seeing that he was now suitably humbled, I allowed him into the Spirit Parlour. "Very nice," he said, running his eye around the room and taking in the draperies, the statues, the hanging lantern and ornate table. "Very exotic. Lots of atmosphere. You do yourself proud, I can see."

I gave him a look, which he returned blandly. "And this is your spirit machine?" he asked, walking over to the table.

"This is the Electrical Spiritograph," I corrected. I couldn't help eyeing it a little nervously, even though I knew it was the dummy. Once bitten, twice shy, as the saying goes, but fortunately it remained uncommunicative.

He bent down to inspect the device with its clock dial and brass trimmings. "Very impressive," he said, straightening up again and drawing out his notebook. "How does it work?"

Assuming my most intellectual manner, I explained about Spirit Energy. He wrote it all down without comment, but equally without any air of believing it.

"So the spirits spell out words on the wheel?"

"Yes, and there's a bell, too, for simple yes and no questions."

"And the spirits do this all by themselves?" he said with a touch of incredulity.

"Through my mediation," I said repressively.

"And would it be possible for me to take your Spiritograph apart, to get a better idea of how it works?"

I told him that he was quite welcome to take it apart, congratulating myself that it was the dummy Spiritograph and would tell him nothing. But he was very quick. A rueful smile touched his lips. "Never mind, Madame Fox. I somehow suspect that would be a waste of time." Casting another look at the table, he said, "Would you be willing to sit down and show me just what happened the other night, as nearly as you can remember?"

I wasn't willing, but I did so. He watched and listened, putting in a question now and then. They were intelligent questions on the whole, and I could tell he wasn't being deliberately offensive, but it was obvious he could not swallow the idea of genuine Spirit Communication. I could not blame him for that. It would have sounded unbelievable to me, too, if I hadn't been there to see it for myself.

"So until this—this spirit spoke through the wheel, you yourself knew nothing about where Miss Langley's body might be?" he asked, for at least the third or fourth time.

"I only knew she was missing," I said patiently. "What her parents told me."

"And what Mr. Herman Price of Price Investigations told you as well?"

It was obvious he thought he was exploding a bombshell. I gazed at him with limpid eyes. "Yes, I thought it best to look thoroughly into the matter before agreeing to sit for the Langleys. If you have been making inquiries about me, you must know that I do not accept all the clients who appeal to me. One would like to help everyone, of course, but one's Powers are unfortunately limited. One is forced to winnow out all but the most desperate, the most worthy—"

"The most wealthy," he said, nodding in agreement.

I drew myself up. "I have not accepted a penny from the Langleys," I said, which was indeed a matter of some grievance to me.

"But there's a reward, isn't there? For information leading to Miss Langley's whereabouts? And you would appear to have earned it."

Astonishingly, this fact had slipped my mind. "I suppose so," I said, rather lamely. "But I was not thinking of the reward when I agreed to sit for the Langleys."

He received this with understandable skepticism. "Yet you represented yourself to Mr. Price as a fellow investigator considering taking the case."

"Yes, I thought it best. So many people have unpleasant ideas about Spiritualists," I said, giving him stare for stare.

He acknowledged this hit with another smile and—to my relief—abandoned the subject. "At any rate, the Langleys don't have any doubts about you and your powers," he said. "The body was in the crypt, just as you said it would be."

"It wasn't I who said it," I said with a little shiver. "And indeed, I am sorry to hear it."

He lowered his notebook to give me a long stare. "I can't make out what you are about," he informed me in a gently complaining voice. "It was your spirit that came through with the information, wasn't it? Isn't that what's supposed to happen?"

All I could do was murmur something about there being Spirits and Spirits and not liking to be mixed up with the police. He was quick, though, Dear Reader—no doubt about it. "A case of the biter bit, was it?" he exclaimed, with a lifted brow. "Got more than you bargained for?"

"I don't know what you mean," I said coldly. "At any rate, this discussion is pointless. You don't believe a word I'm saying."

"I might," he said. He hesitated a moment, giving me a sidelong look. "I've reason to be skeptical of what you might call professional spiritualists. You must know yourself that there are some unprincipled people out there going by that name. But at the same time, I'm willing to believe there are things that can't be explained by ordinary means. In fact, I had an experience of that kind myself."

"Did you?" I asked, in spite of my resolution not to encourage him.

"I did. I had a dog years ago. I was very attached to that dog. He always slept on the hearthrug in my bedroom. Well, he grew old, and one day he died—as dogs will, even the best of them. And that same night, as I was lying there in bed, I heard his nails come clicking down the hall, into my room, and over to the hearth, just as they used to. But when I sat up and looked, there wasn't anything there." He gave me an embarrassed smile. "I've never told anyone about it until now. I knew they wouldn't believe me. They'd say I dreamed it. But it really happened. So if you insist, I'm willing to believe that the spirit of poor Miss Langley came to you the other night and told you where to find her body."

From this point on, the atmosphere between us became more relaxed, Dear Reader—indeed, almost friendly. I invited him back into the Sitting Room, where we resumed our seats, and he proceeded to give me the details of how Miss Langley's body had been found.

"There's an old church, not too far from where the Langleys live. The place was abandoned a long time ago. The roof's entirely gone and the glass out of the windows, but there's a crypt right enough. And that's where she was."

I told him that I had seen the church in question on the occasion of my visit to the Arbours. "But how curious that the body should be in a crypt," I said. "That seems a most mysterious circumstance. Indeed, it is quite as mysterious as her disappearing in the first place. For someone to go through the ritual of burying her formally—"

"Ah, but it wasn't a formal burial. The body wasn't in a coffin or sepulcher. It wasn't even in the crypt proper. Not too long ago, apparently, you could have put it down there without too much trouble, but the local police superintendent told me that the whole undercroft caved in a few years ago. Right before Miss Langley disappeared, as it happens."

"So the ground would have been disturbed already, if someone was looking for an inconspicuous place to hide a body?"

"Exactly," said the Inspector, with an approving nod. "No one would have noticed a spot of fresh ground turned over—and in fact nobody did. But after your séance the other night, the Langleys hired a party of workmen to do some digging around the church, and they found Miss Langley's body in the old stairway leading down to the crypt."

"Was she murdered?" I asked in a low voice. That was the question that had been haunting me all the while.

He cocked an eyebrow at me. "Well, it took a fair amount of digging to find the body. It stands to reason she didn't bury herself. But at the same time, the medical gentlemen didn't find anything to indicate exactly how she died. It's been three years, after all, with her in the ground all the time as it now appears. So her death might conceivably have been suicide or accident—if you're willing to believe somebody came along afterwards and buried her. I don't believe in that sort of coincidence myself, but it's just possible."

This made me shiver, too. "Poor creature. I wonder what happened to her."

"Yes, so do I. I was hoping you might be able to help me with that."

I demurred at once, and with emphasis. "I have told you all I know, Inspector."

"Perhaps you have. What I'd like to know now is what you suspect." Putting down his notebook, he gave me a disarming smile. "I've been impressed by what I've seen of you, Madame Fox. You're clearly a clever woman and have—er—seen a bit of the world. And frankly speaking, without you we'd probably never have found out what happened to Miss Langley."

This was flattering, Dear Reader, but I still had no wish to be drawn into a police affair. "I can't see that my suspicions would be the least use to you," I said.

"You never know. For instance, I'd be interested in hearing what you thought of young Roland. I will tell you in confidence that in a case of this sort, nine times out of ten we find it's a husband or lover who's responsible."

"He seemed pleasant enough," I said cautiously. "A trifle effete, perhaps. But in any case, certainly not the type to commit murder."

He shook his head. "Ah, but one of the things we learn in the force is that given the right motive and circumstances, nearly any-body's a potential killer. Murder's one of the most democratic of crimes." He gave me a conspiratorial smile. "People like you and me, now, Madame Fox—we'd never dream of breaking into a bank, or stealing someone's purse. But in the right circumstances—if we were fighting for our life, say, or for someone or something we cared deeply about—we might kill."

"But in that case it would be manslaughter rather than murder, would it not?"

He laughed. "I said you were clever! Yes, depending on the cir-cumstances, it might be. But the principle holds true down the line. I agree Mr. Roland doesn't seem the type to murder, but he's still at the top of my list of suspects. How did he react when your wheel spelled out 'crypt'?"

Frowning, I tried to remember. "I don't believe he *said* anything. We none of us said a word until the wheel stopped moving. When it was done spelling 'crypt,' Mrs. Langley suggested it might mean the old church crypt. Mr. Roland didn't say anything to that, either. And his face isn't particularly expressive—and I'm afraid at that point I wasn't paying much attention to him anyway. I think the only time he spoke during the sitting was when the wheel spelled 'sin.' He spoke the word aloud, as if it were a question—and the bell rang, as if it were answering him."

"The answer being 'yes,' I take it? That's another thing I wanted to ask you about. What did you make of this mention of sin?"

"I didn't like it," I said at once. "I have wondered about it since. Whether it were referring to murder, or to something else. "

He nodded, as though pleased by my response. "I've been wondering about that, too. Mr. Roland didn't seem to draw an association with any particular sin?"

"No, both he and Mrs. Langley seemed puzzled."

He pounced at once on my omission. "And what about Mr. Langley?"

Again I tried to remember. "He didn't say anything. That's all I remember. He didn't say anything at all until it was over." I regarded the Inspector with interest. "Do you have a reason for suspecting Mr. Langley?"

"No particular reason. Of course he's not what you'd call a likely suspect. Fathers do kill daughters now and again, but not normally fathers of his class. And not without something more of a motive than we've been able to turn up. He seemed genuinely broken up about finding her dead. What did you think?"

"He seemed very shaken," I said, shutting my eyes to better recollect. "In fact, as soon as the—the phenomena started happening, he was *literally* shaking. I was holding his hand, so I know. It was genuine emotion, I feel sure—although of course, I can't be sure exactly *what* emotion. I'm bound to say he was opposed to my getting involved in the business in the beginning. And that tended to arouse my suspicions, but you must make allowance for that. I might not be quite fair, owing to his initial hostility."

Inspector Harper promised he would make all due allowances and scribbled a few words in his notebook. "To return to Mr. Roland, now. You are inclined to consider him guiltless of having any hand in Miss Langley's death?"

I hesitated before speaking. "Not exactly," I said. "I can't believe he had any hand directly. But I could imagine he might have driven the poor girl to suicide under the right circumstances. Entirely without meaning to, you understand."

The Inspector regarded me with raised eyebrows. "Whatever do you mean?"

I tried to explain what I meant. "When I spoke to him, he seemed to have a very idealized picture of Miss Langley. He saw her as an angel, not a woman. If she were to have done something that she knew would injure his idealized image of her . . . if she *had* committed some sin, in fact . . .." My voice trailed off.

Inspector Harper regarded me for some moments without speaking. "That's a very interesting theory," he said at last. "And an original theory, too. I've been on this case practically since the beginning, but I have to admit such an idea never occurred to me. Of course, it wouldn't account for Miss Langley's body being buried." He stopped to think for a moment. "But if, as you say, she *had* committed some sin—and you must forgive my policeman's mind if I jump to the conclusion that it was what you might call a sin of the flesh—she must have committed it *with* someone. And if it wasn't with young Roland—"

"The other suitor," I said at once. "The one Mr. Roland said was only a childhood friend. I can't recall the name—"

"Stern," he said. "Jim Stern. Yes, indeed! He's the other name at the top of my list. If he and Miss Langley had been lovers, and she thought Mr. Roland was going to find out, she might have committed suicide. And Stern buried her to cover it up? Because he was afraid of the scandal? No, that doesn't seem enough of a motive." Again he thought for a moment. "Perhaps Stern was blackmailing her, threatening to tell Roland. And then she commits suicide—leaving a note, perhaps, explaining why. And Stern destroys the note and hides her body because he doesn't want his part in the business to come out. Yes, that could be it. I had been inclined to put Stern at the head of the list anyway, because Miss Langley had refused to marry him—or her parents had refused him. At any rate, it's all one. That's motive enough for murder right there."

"In that case, Mr. Roland has an equal motive," I pointed out. "Because she was refusing to marry him, too."

The Inspector's eyes nearly popped out of his head. "She was refusing to marry *Roland*?"

"Yes," I said. "Though of course Roland was too obtuse to see it that way. He thought it was just maidenly modesty."

The Inspector drew a deep breath. "You'd better tell me all about it. I must say, this is the first I've heard of it. Roland said nothing whatever to the police about the engagement being broken."

I gave him the gist of my conversation with Mr. Roland, but he asked so many questions, and kept wanting me to recall the exact words Roland had used, that I told him it might be better if I just let him read the transcript. "You made a *transcript* of the conversation?" he said, looking flabbergasted.

I said vaguely that in this particular case, I had thought it best to do so. In fact, Dear Reader, it was my usual practice. During interviews with prospective clients, Susan stays within earshot and writes down everything that is said. I have a good memory, but I can't be expected to know what information might turn out to be valuable in the future. You may have already gathered that in my business, information is currency, or at least directly translatable to such.

Inspector Harper read through the transcript of my interview with Mr. Roland, exclaiming at intervals that Roland had never said any of this to the police. "I tell you what: we ought to get you on the force, Madame Fox," he said. "To think of your getting such admissions from him!"

I was pleased by his praise, but pointed out that Mr. Roland would scarcely have spoken so freely if I had been an official agent of the police.

"Perhaps not. But it's evident you have a sympathetic manner. When you want to," he added, with a wry smile.

I smiled back, but told him I felt a little uneasy about betraying Mr. Roland's confidences. "Yes, I daresay," he said. "But it's information we needed. It gives us at least a couple of new lines to try. I'd like to make a copy of this transcript, if I may."

Since I was sure he was only putting it in the form of a request to be polite, I made no objection to his copying the transcript. "Thank you," he said, when he was done and preparing to take his leave. "It's been a pleasure meeting you, Madame Fox. Kindly let us know if you learn anything else that might have a bearing on the case. You have my card, haven't you? Just send me word, and I can come around directly."

I told him firmly that that was not in the least likely. "Oh, you never know," he said, as he stepped out the door. "I don't pretend to have your powers, but I have a strong presentiment we're likely to meet again over this business!"

CHAPTER 6

Susan was relieved to hear that my interview with the Inspector had gone so smoothly. "He wasn't at all a bad sort, for a policeman," I said. "On the whole, I think I scraped through reasonably well. Let's wait a few more days, and if nothing else happens, we might think about starting up the business again."

Alas, it was not to be. Less than forty-eight hours after my interview with Inspector Harper, Susan came to tell me there was another gentleman to see me. "A Mr. James Stern," she said. "And a Miss Stern, too."

"Just one thing after another," I said bitterly. "What on earth do they want?"

"They didn't say, but the young gentleman looks upset-like. The young lady not so much—she kept giggling and gawking around as if she was at a raree show. I put them both in the Sitting Room."

I supposed I could deny myself, but in some obscure way I felt obliged to see the Sterns. It was as if it were a penance laid on me. Or perhaps it was merely curiosity, of which I will admit to having my fair share. Inspector Harper had said Mr. Stern was at the top of his list of suspects. I thought I would like to see for myself the young man who might or might not have been Miss Langley's partner in sin as well as her murderer.

I had second thoughts about this as soon as I entered the Sitting Room. With a lowering brow, he sprang to his feet and bounded forward as if he were intending to murder *me*.

"You!" he exclaimed in aggressive accents. "What do you mean by telling the police I killed Elizabeth Langley?"

Although I recoiled instinctively from this accusation, I soon recovered myself. "I beg your pardon," I said, with chilly dignity. "I don't believe I have the pleasure of your acquaintance, sir."

"Don't be a bear, Jim," said Miss Stern, giggling. "You always do fly off the handle."

Mr. Stern flushed. "I beg your pardon," he said stiffly. "My name is James Stern, ma'am. And this is my sister Cora."

As I made a conventional response to their greetings, I surveyed them both with interest. Mr. Stern was a sturdy young man, less handsome than Mr. Roland but attractive nonetheless. He had springy chestnut curls and a sun-browned complexion. This, together with the cut of his jacket and his handkerchief tie, made it obvious he was a sporting man—although boy might have been the more accurate term. He appeared scarcely out of his teens.

Miss Stern, whom I judged to be a year or two older, also had springy chestnut curls, which she wore dressed in ringlets down her back. A giddy hat trimmed with pansies was perched atop her head in the gravity-defying style that is currently fashionable. Her mauve crepe-de-chine dress was flounced and beribboned and trimmed with yards of lace, and so was her matching sunshade. She stared at me with open interest, her eyes flickering from my rings to my veil to my jet-trimmed dress of black bombazine.

"I was so eager to meet you, Madame Fox," she said in a gushing voice. "When Jim said he was coming to see you, I simply insisted on coming along. Isn't this business of Elizabeth Langley simply too *horrid?*"

Her brother winced. "Don't, Cora," he said.

"But Jim, it *is* horrid! And you know she was one of my closest friends." Miss Stern pursed her lips and wrinkled her pretty forehead in a semblance of grief. "I was never so shocked in my life as when I heard what had happened. To think that she was there in the church crypt all this time. Is it true that you told the police where her body was, Madame Fox?"

"Don't, Cora," said her brother again. There was bewildered unhappiness in his eyes as he looked at me. "I apologize again for speaking to you as I did, ma'am. I should not have done so. But hearing about Elizabeth was shock enough, without the police harassing me as they have done." His voice sharpened as he added, "Indeed, it's outside of enough that I should be suspected of killing her, when I loved her. For I did love her," he repeated, looking at me defiantly. "I had nothing to do with her death. Nothing!"

"It's true," said Miss Stern, nodding vigourously. "He had nothing to do with it."

"And I'd like to know what reason you have for saying I did," he continued.

"Did the Spirits say so?" interpolated his sister with bright curiosity.

By this time, I was wishing I had seen them separately, Dear Reader. It was difficult to keep up with this double-barreled blast of questions. Instead of trying to reply, I invited them to sit down and gave a brief account of my rôle in the investigation, stressing that I had made no accusation against Mr. Stern, but suppressing the fact that I had supplied the police with a motive for him.

He received my words skeptically. "But the police obviously think I had something to do with it. The inspector I talked to kept asking the same questions, as if he thought I knew more than I was telling him."

Miss Stern reacted differently. "That's simply too *eerie*! I have always felt there was something in Spiritualism. Indeed, I have been told I have mediumistic abilities myself."

Again, I felt I was losing control of the conversation. "You both knew Miss Langley?" I asked, trying to divert the flow into a channel of my own choosing. "Had you known her long?"

Mr. Stern opened his mouth to reply, but Miss Stern was quicker. "Oh, yes," she said. "Elizabeth was one of my closest friends."

Somehow, I doubted that. I have seen enough genuine grief to know it when I see it, and I didn't detect any in Miss Stern's manner. What I did see was a desire to make herself interesting by exaggerating her connection with a girl who had met a tragic end. Mr. Stern I was inclined to credit with a more genuine feeling, but of course I couldn't be sure. "How long had you known her?" I repeated.

"Oh, we grew up together! We all used to play together as children. Our families' properties adjoin, you see."

I encouraged her to enlarge on this subject. What she said confirmed my suspicions. There had been a superficial kind of friendship between the Sterns and their young neighbour, but little real affinity—between the two girls, at least. "Elizabeth was a dear girl, but rather *backward*," explained Miss Stern. "I always thought it was her growing up in India. She was such a timid little thing, afraid of her own shadow. The least little thing would make her cry."

"That's not quite fair, Cora," put in her brother. "She was sensitive, but hardly backward."

"Naturally you would say so, Jim," retorted his sister. "But for a girl of her age, she really was incredibly naïve, Madame Fox. Her parents had positively kept her in cotton wool."

This was interesting, but I didn't see that it was going to help determine Mr. Stern's rôle in her death. "I had gathered her parents rather indulged her," I said. "But something seems to have been troubling her all the same, toward the end."

"Something was *always* troubling her," said Miss Stern dismissively.

"But in this case, it seems to have been something serious. Something that might perhaps have had a bearing on her death."

Miss Stern looked interested. "Do you mean she had a premonition she was going to die?"

"No, that's not what I meant. Did she confide in you? Tell you her secrets?" I asked, putting the question directly.

"No," admitted Miss Stern, with obvious reluctance. "We had not really spoken in years. Especially after Jim proposed to her and she turned him down. Of course, I could not like to be friends with her after *that*."

Mr. Stern was looking unhappy. "She did not turn me down," he said. "It was her parents who did that. They thought I wasn't good enough for her. Or at least not *rich* enough for her."

Miss Stern gave him a pitying look. "Oh, Jim! I don't think her parents would have objected, if she had really wanted to marry you. They gave her anything she wanted, as far as I could see."

He shook his head stubbornly. "I don't think so. Not about this. When I spoke to her father, he turned me down flat and wouldn't even let me speak to her."

I pricked up my ears at these words. "But she knew that you were proposing to marry her?"

He hesitated, then nodded reluctantly. "Yes, I told her beforehand."

"And she gave you reason to think your feelings were returned?"

Again he hesitated. "Yes, I am sure she cared for me. Although she was very modest—"

"*Backward*," mouthed Miss Stern.

"—I would never have offered for her if I had not thought my feelings were returned."

"And when did this offer take place?" I asked. "I assume it was before she accepted Mr. Roland's proposal?"

"Yes, it was more than a year before that," said Mr. Stern. "But not so very much more." Rather bitterly, he added, "According to her parents, she was far too young to marry *me*. But they didn't have any qualms about accepting Roland's suit only a year later."

"That must have been a great disappointment to you," I said.

He flushed. "Yes, it was. But I didn't kill her!"

"Who do you think did?"

Again he shook his head, this time with an air of bewilderment. "I cannot imagine who would have wanted to hurt her."

"Of course the police are inclined to suspect husbands or lovers in this kind of case," I said, watching him closely.

I thought he might react to the mention of lovers, if he and Miss Langley had indeed had some kind of physical relationship. But he only said, "Roland, do you mean? I cannot like him, but I don't believe he would be capable of this kind of crime." He considered the idea anew, then shook his head with decision. "No, surely not. It seems most unlikely."

"Perhaps it was a tramp," suggested Miss Stern. "I saw a nasty-looking fellow just the other day, hanging about in the lane. He looked as if he were capable of anything. And you hear such horrid stories sometimes—"

Again her brother winced. "Don't, Cora," he said.

"Well, I should think a tramp was more likely than poor Giles Roland. He's such a lamb, Madame Fox. I'll never believe he had anything to do with it."

As far as I could tell, we didn't appear to be getting anywhere. "Did Elizabeth have other friends?" I asked. "Some girl or woman she might have confided in?"

Mr. and Miss Stern exchanged glances. "She had an ayah," said Mr. Stern, rather doubtfully. "An Indian nursemaid."

"Oh, that was *ages* ago, Jim," said Miss Stern. "The ayah went back to India when Elizabeth was still quite a child. Don't you remember how upset she was about it? She cried and cried. You would have thought the world was ending," she added with a sniff.

"How long ago was this?" I asked. It didn't sound as if it had any bearing on the case, but Miss Stern was such an unreliable witness that I was unsure what her definition of "quite a child" might be.

Neither Miss Stern nor Mr. Stern were able to pinpoint exactly when the ayah had gone back to India, but both seemed sure that Elizabeth could have been no older than nine or ten at the time.

"Did she have another nurse after the ayah left?" I asked, still hoping to learn of some confidante who might shed light on Miss Langley's state of mind.

"No, she had a governess—Miss Pring."

"And was she as close to this governess as she was to her ayah?"

Again the Sterns exchanged glances. "I shouldn't think so," said Miss Stern.

"No, indeed," said Mr. Stern, quite definitely. "Miss Pring wasn't at all the sort of woman you'd make a bosom-bow of. Don't you remember how she used to scold, Cora, when we came over during Elizabeth's lesson times? Or almost any other time, for that matter. We called her Miss Prunes-and-Prisms," he added with a reminiscent smile. "I know Elizabeth was glad to see the last of her."

"And when did she leave?" I asked, with only faint hopes that I might yet be on the trail of a promising lead.

"Oh, ages ago," said Miss Stern. "It was about the time I went off to Miss Broadman's Academy. I think Elizabeth was sixteen at the time."

This was disappointing, Dear Reader, but after all no more than I might have expected. The police had already spoken to Mr. Stern several times without learning anything of interest. I realized I must have let the Inspector's words of praise go to my head if I were imagining I might be able to do better.

So I brought the interview to an end as soon as I could, although I had first to give Miss Stern an account of my séance with the Langleys. I found myself skimming over the mention of sin. It would have been different if Miss Stern had really been a friend to Miss Langley, but it was obvious she had been nothing of the kind. I felt oddly protective of poor Miss Langley and reluctant to expose her secret to such prurient interest.

Even as it was, Miss Stern shivered and exclaimed and said it was all too eerie, really. Her brother merely sat in stricken silence throughout my narrative. When it was over, however, he surprised me by asking if there was something I wasn't telling. "From what the inspector said, I gathered there was something that happened at the séance that implicated *me*."

"He told you that?" I said. Privately, I was amazed that Inspector Harper would have been so forthcoming. Giving public credit to the utterances of a Spiritualist did not seem in accordance with Scotland Yard policy. It was flattering if it were true, of course, but I could not help wondering if the Inspector might have had some deeper motive.

Aloud, I said, "I can assure you that your name was not mentioned at all, Mr. Stern, at least during the sitting. Mr. Roland did mention you casually beforehand, but that was the only time your name came up."

The mention of his successful rival made Mr. Stern's face tighten. "What did Roland say about me?" he demanded.

"He said you were a childhood friend of Miss Langley—nothing more."

Mr. Stern made a noise like a snort. "Did he dare suggest I murdered her?"

"No, not at all. He was convinced some accident had befallen her."

He still seemed unsatisfied, but his sister got up, saying she had errands to run and they must be leaving. "Will you sit again for the Langleys?" she asked as Susan showed her and her brother to the door. "I would love to be present if you do!"

"They will not want me to," I said with finality. That first sitting had been sufficiently disquieting, and look what trouble it had created for all of us. I was certain the Langleys wished as little as I to undergo another sitting with the Electrical Spiritograph.

CHAPTER 7

A s it happened, I was mistaken. The very next day, Mrs. Langley came to call on me, and I learned that despite our disquieting first sitting, she looked upon me as a True Oracle (which was gratifying) and a possible source of further revelations (which was not).

"My dear Madame Fox, I can never thank you enough," she said, pressing my hand between her own. Dressed now in deepest mourning, she took a seat beside me on my Sitting Room sofa. Fixing me with her large, light blue eyes, she continued, "You had my letter, of course. But I felt I had to come and thank you in person."

I was surprised to hear she had written me, Dear Reader. It was, after all, Inspector Harper who had told me the sad result of the search. I could recall Mrs. Langley assuring me after the sitting that she would send me word herself, but the lack of such word had not disturbed me. Indeed, I had thought it quite natural that after such a shocking turn of events she might have forgotten all about her promise.

I said as much to Mrs. Langley, but she frowned at my words. "You did not receive my letter?" she repeated. "How very odd. For I most certainly wrote to you! But of course we were all at sixes and sevens after learning of—of Elizabeth's being found. And then again, in making the arrangements afterwards. I daresay I may have gotten your direction wrong, or made some other such mistake, in the confusion."

She seemed satisfied that this was the explanation, and indeed it seemed quite plausible. Yet all the same, Dear Reader, I felt a pricking in my thumbs. Here was another mystery, and though quite a minor one in itself, I could not help wondering if it had a bearing on the other.

Meanwhile, Mrs. Langley was telling me how and where they had found her daughter's body. I had already had these details from Inspector Harper, but I felt there might be a therapeutic value in letting her talk about them. Poor lady, it was little enough I could do to comfort her. Yet she assured me over and over that despite the sad outcome, she was very grateful to know her daughter's fate. "If it were not for you, I feel sure we would never have known. And the uncertainty would have driven me mad."

I could understand that and told her I was glad to have been of help. "I hope the police will soon uncover the whole story of what happened," I said. "And then you will be truly at rest—or as much as you can be, in such sad circumstances."

She shook her head slowly. "Perhaps so," she said. "But it seems a most unfathomable mystery. Who would have wanted to hurt Elizabeth? I ask myself over and over, and yet I can think of no one."

Uncomfortable under her searching, sad-eyed gaze, I said again, awkwardly, that the police would doubtless soon cast light on the matter.

"The police!" she repeated. "I daresay. Though of course nothing they or anyone else can do will bring Elizabeth back. That is what my husband says, and I do admit the point, though I still feel there would be a comfort in knowing the culprit was brought to justice. But my husband says that is unlikely after all this time. And what will searching for the culprit avail us, if all it does is alienate our neighbours and yet return no result?"

I wondered if she was referring to the Sterns. "It's natural that the police should pay particular attention to the people who were closest to your daughter," I said. "And seeing that she was found so near to home, of course your neighbours would come in for their share of questioning. One hopes they would understand that and not take it amiss."

"Yes, to be sure," said Mrs. Langley. "But I cannot like it, and I am sure they do not like it, either."

"Does the investigation seem to be focusing on anyone in particular?"

She nodded. "Yes, from one or two things the police inspector told me, I rather gathered that they suspect Jim Stern. Poor Jim! I am certain he can have had nothing to do with it. Indeed, I am at a loss to know why the police think he might."

Why they thought he might was no mystery to me, of course. "I understood it was because he was a suitor of your daughter's," I said. "And an unsuccessful suitor at that. The police probably think he bore her a grudge on that account."

"A suitor?" she said, shaking her head once again. "I suppose he might be called that. But as for being unsuccessful—well, that is hardly the proper term, to my way of thinking. He did make an offer for Elizabeth years ago, but they were both hardly more than children at the time. Mr. Langley told him he must wait a year or two, and then, if both he and Elizabeth were still of the same mind, we might consider it."

This was so different from the version Mr. Stern had told me that I could only stare. It was nearly a full minute before I managed to say, in a careful voice, "Mr. Stern told me he was rejected because he was not sufficiently rich."

"I don't know why he would say that," she said, looking puzzled. "He is perhaps not as well-to-do as Mr. Roland, but his father owns a very respectable property in the neighbourhood. And Jim is his only son and his heir. Perhaps he misunderstood?"

"Perhaps so," I said, but the pricking in my thumbs had grown stronger. It seemed Mr. Stern had lied. If he had lied about a small matter, he might have lied about a larger one. My mind was working furiously as Mrs. Langley went on talking about her daughter's friendship with both the Stern children.

"I like Jim very well, but between you and me, I never could really like Cora. I don't think there is any real harm in the girl, but she was a bit older than Elizabeth and rather inclined to bully her. I remember Elizabeth often coming home in tears after spending the day with her."

I nodded sympathetically. "I gathered Elizabeth was a sensitive child."

"Yes, she was," said Mrs. Langley. Her lip quivered. "I think about it now and wonder if we did wrong, raising her as we did. Of course we meant it for the best. But from the moment she was born, she was our darling, the apple of our eye. Indeed, she was the sunniest, most delightful creature—but inclined to be headstrong, as only children often are. I am afraid my husband and I indulged her too much, and so did her ayah."

I nodded again at the mention of Elizabeth's Indian nursemaid. "I understood the ayah went back to India, though?"

"Yes, when Elizabeth was nine. Poor Reema, she was not very happy here. I believe the English servants treated her unkindly. And of course, after India, she must have found the climate dreadfully cold. But Elizabeth was very distressed to see her go. Poor Elizabeth! If it had been left to me, I don't think I could have insisted, but my husband argued that she was growing spoiled, and it might be better to have her under the care of an Englishwoman—someone who would not only undertake her education, but provide her with the discipline that we ourselves were unable to give her."

I remembered the Sterns' disparaging remarks about Miss Langley's governess. "How did that answer?" I asked curiously.

Mrs. Langley took a little time replying. "I am not sure it answered at all," she said at last. "Reema had been less a servant to my daughter than a friend—or indeed an older sister. They had been together from the time Elizabeth was born. Literally together, I mean, for Reema had slept in the nursery and shared her meals and play. Miss Pring, on the other hand, felt Elizabeth was getting too old for nursery treatment. She was a very strict, not very imaginative woman with set ideas about lessons, and play, and meals. It was a complete contrast from Reema's regime, and there were some terrible scenes. Nighttime was the worst. Elizabeth was afraid of the dark, yet Miss Pring insisted that she be made to sleep alone, without a light."

Slow tears were rolling down Mrs. Langley's face now. "My poor girl," she cried. "I keep thinking of that now. Of her alone in the dark and afraid."

I did what I could to comfort her, ringing for Susan to bring hartshorn, along with some wine and water. With the help of these aids, Mrs. Langley eventually mastered herself, though she could not seem to let the subject go.

"Ever since her body was found, I keep thinking of how Elizabeth feared being alone in the dark. In the end, I simply could not bear the thought of burying her. It was bad enough that she had been alone in the earth so long. As soon as the police released her to us, I had her body cremated. I know some of our neighbours thought it very dreadful, but cremation was quite common in India and a sensible practice, I have always thought. In any case, I am happier knowing Elizabeth is not lying in the cold earth."

Remembering the dank earthen smell that had pervaded the Spirit Parlour on the night of the séance, I heartily endorsed these sentiments. Mrs. Langley gave me a trembling smile. "And I hope her spirit is at rest now—but do you think it can be, Madame Fox? For her murderer is still at large, you know. I am not, I hope, a vindictive woman, but that thought troubles me."

I thought I could see where this was leading. "Your best hope for that," I said as firmly as possible, "is the police."

"I have no faith in the police," she returned. "In three years, they found no trace of Elizabeth. How can I have faith that they will find her murderer?"

I told her that was quite a different thing. "Before, it was a question of whether a crime had even been committed. The police are naturally at a disadvantage in that case, for it is difficult to prove a negative. But now that we know there was a crime, the police have faculties to investigate the matter far better than anyone else. Although—" I hesitated, trying to put the subject as delicately as I could, "—although it's just possible they may find it was not the crime we think. Have you ever considered, ma'am, that she might not have been murdered? That she might perhaps have taken her own life?"

"The police did suggest it was a possibility," said Mrs. Langley, looking troubled. "But I cannot imagine why my daughter would have done such a thing. And there is the fact that her body was apparently buried. Why would that be, if it were suicide?"

Obviously, the Inspector had not mentioned the Jim Stern-as-lover-and-possible-blackmailer theory. I did not feel it was my place to mention it, either, especially since Miss Langley's mother would doubtless find it a very shocking and painful theory. At the same time, however, there would be a benefit to us all if we could resolve the business. In an attempt to approach the subject in a roundabout way, I said, "I only wondered, because apparently something was troubling Miss Langley in the days prior to her disappearance. Mr. Roland spoke of her wishing to break her engagement."

Mrs. Langley shook her head. "The police inspector mentioned that, but I find it difficult to believe. She was sincerely attached to Mr. Roland, and he to her, I am sure. They were a very well-matched couple. Much as I liked Jim Stern, I did not think he and Elizabeth were nearly as well-suited."

"Temperamentally, you mean?"

"Yes, exactly that. Jim is a nice boy, but still very much a boy in his ways—a trifle heedless and thoughtless. Not only that, but like so many boys, he is mad about sport to the exclusion of almost everything else. Nothing that time will not cure, you understand, but to my mind he is still too young for marriage, and I suspect his parents feel the same."

"Did they say so?" I asked, alert to any hint of further motive.

"No, I understand they made no objection at the time he proposed for her."

"So the reservations were all on your side—yours and your husband's?"

"Yes," she said. "But not merely on account of Mr. Stern. Indeed, our qualms were rather more centred around Elizabeth. She was young for her age, and I was not convinced that she really loved Jim Stern—not as a woman should love her husband-to-be. Like so many girls, she had a headful of romantic ideas about love and marriage, but little idea of what being married really entailed."

"And did you tell her?" I asked. Of course what I really wished to know was whether she had discussed what Mr. Roland had called "the physical aspects of marriage" with her daughter.

Mrs. Langley smiled. "I did not. As I say, Elizabeth was very young, and I thought it better not to—well, to brush the bloom away, if you will. The innocence of girlhood is a very precious thing. It vanishes all too soon in any case."

I said nothing, Dear Reader, for in fact I did not agree with her. I know it is the fashion at present to keep young women ignorant of the so-called facts of life, right up till their marriage day, in the name of preserving their innocence. Yet there are occasions when a little specific knowledge might keep those same young women out of danger: a danger into which innocence might all too easily stray. I wondered if this had been Miss Langley's experience.

"I suppose," I said, watching Mrs. Langley closely, "with your daughter's marriage to Mr. Roland so near, you would have had to enlighten her soon, if you had not already."

I was not prepared for the look that appeared on Mrs. Langley's face. "Oh," she said, and then again, "Oh!"

I was perfectly sure these words presaged some important revelation. I literally held my breath, waiting to hear what she could have remembered that had affected her so strongly.

Eventually I had to give in and start breathing again, even without having my curiosity satisfied. For it seemed as if Mrs. Langley had forgotten I was there. She sat silently, her brow contracted in thought, her eyes fixed absently on her black-gloved hands.

Finally, just when I had made up my mind that she was not going to tell me, she looked up with a strained expression. "You are quite right," she said. "I had forgotten, Madame Fox."

This would have been gratifying, except I was unsure exactly what I was right about. Fortunately, her next words enlightened me. "I had talked to Elizabeth not long before her disappearance, about—about the duties of the marital state. I did not associate the two, for her disappearance occurred some days later. But I do recall her being—not distraught, exactly. And not exactly shocked, I think.

Indeed, she said very little. But even at the time, I wondered. Her expression was so . . . peculiar."

I longed to know exactly what Mrs. Langley had said, and exactly how her daughter had responded. But it was doubtful that she had had the foresight to make a written transcript of the conversation, or that she would have been willing to let me read it even if she had. "It's not to be wondered at if she was a *little* shocked," I said, with spurious cheer. "Being such an innocent girl, as you say."

Mrs. Langley agreed, but with a hesitant air. "That might account for it, perhaps. I know I tried to reassure her. I told her that Mr. Roland was a good Christian gentleman and would undoubtedly make every allowance for her natural scruples. Indeed, he would value them as tokens of her purity of mind and body."

I felt quite sure Mr. Roland would. He, too, had talked of natural scruples and purity in the same high-flown and idealistic way. Still, words and deeds are not necessarily the same thing. Sometimes a gentleman will espouse the most exalted feelings for a woman, when what he actually has in mind is a very earthy (not to say fleshly) relationship. I have encountered many such in Spiritualistic circles. Unfortunately, there seems to be a common misconception that any woman calling herself a Spiritualist must also be an adherent of Free Love.

Whatever you may think of my morals, Dear Reader, I can assure you that I never had any truck with Free Love. It has always been my belief that Love, like nearly everything else, prospers best on a sound business footing. But there are plenty of women—and intelligent women, too—who have been seduced first figuratively and then actually by the doctrine of Free Love. I could not help wondering if Elizabeth Langley might have been among them.

In any case, it seemed too much of a coincidence that so soon after learning of her future husband's marital expectations, she had first made an effort to break her engagement and then had vanished altogether.

Mrs. Langley seemed to feel the sequence of events suggestive also, though the conclusions she drew were not exactly the same as mine. "Even if Elizabeth were troubled by what I told her—even if she decided she did not want to marry—there would have been no reason for her to take her own life," she said, sounding as if she were trying to convince herself as much as me.

"Perhaps she felt she could not draw back honourably from her engagement with Mr. Roland?" I suggested.

Mrs. Langley's first impulse was to deny this possibility. After turning it over in her mind, however, she admitted it was possible. "Of course we would have supported her, no matter what she chose to do. But there is no doubt that breaking an engagement is a serious matter. And it had been announced in the newspapers, so it would have been a public matter, not merely a private one. She might have felt she was shaming us by wanting to back out at such a late date."

The idea obviously distressed her, but she soon recalled that her daughter's body had been concealed after death. "I cannot think why that would have happened if she took her own life," she said. "Why would anyone bury her, unless it were to conceal his own guilt?"

Once again, I did not feel it my place to suggest that guilt in this case might not mean guilt of murder, but rather guilt for having harried Miss Langley to suicide through some lesser crime like blackmail or extortion. As it was, I felt I had been harrying my own victim quite long enough. When I sought to bring the interview to a close, however, Mrs. Langley told me she had another reason for calling on me besides merely to thank me. I had suspected as much early on, of course, and had been trying to divert her, but there was no keeping her from making her request.

"I would like to arrange another sitting, Madame Fox. I want to know who was responsible for my daughter's death. Even if there is no evidence to convict him, I want to know."

Again I protested that the matter was in the hands of the police and had better be left there. Mrs. Langley said again that she had no opinion of the police, but (on the contrary) a very high opinion of me and my powers.

"That is very kind of you, ma'am, but still I must refuse," I told her. "I am sure I could do nothing."

"Ah, you said as much in the beginning, but you see how wrong you were. You found my daughter. Cannot you find her murderer as well?"

I did not know if I could, Dear Reader, but I knew I did not want to try. The thought of another session in the Spirit Parlour where I was not the Moving Spirit made me feel distinctly ill. I said the police would not like my meddling in the affair—a statement I felt was probably true. Mrs. Langley, however, jumped to the conclusion that my scruples were money-related.

"Of course I would pay you for your trouble," she said earnestly. "You have already earned the reward we were offering for information about Elizabeth's whereabouts. If you were successful in this as well, I would be willing to double it."

I said that money was not the issue. I marveled to find such words on my lips. Still more marvelous was the fact that I was speaking the truth.

"What is the issue, then?" she wanted to know.

Since truth-speaking seemed the order of the day, I settled on a modified version thereof. "You know yourself what a shattering experience our last sitting was. I tell you frankly that I am still not recovered from it. Indeed, I shrink from undergoing such an experience again. I would so much rather allow the police to find the culprit in the ordinary way." I was then inspired to add a warning, one I was peculiarly fitted to make: "Then, too, I must caution you against putting too much faith in Spiritualism, ma'am. It can certainly bring comfort, but it can be dangerous, too. There is a danger of obsession—of turning one's eyes to the past, when true hope and happiness must lie in the future."

Squeezing my hand warmly, Mrs. Langley said that she respected my scruples. "Of course I will not press you, Madame Fox," she said. "But equally of course, you must know how I long to uncover the truth in this matter. So if the police fail to find the culprit, you must prepare yourself for my coming to ask you again. And I hope at that time, you will be willing to give me a different answer than you have today."

CHAPTER 8

Almost before Susan had shut the door behind Mrs. Langley, she burst into speech. "I never thought to see the day," she said.

"What day is that?" I asked, rather snappishly.

"The day I hear you turning down a fat commission. And the day I hear you lecturing against putting too much faith in Spiritualism!"

"I suppose there must be a first time for everything," I said. My head was aching again; I put my hands to my throbbing temples. "Let us hope there won't be many more such days. I wish the police would bestir themselves and solve this damnable mystery, so I can get on with my own proper business."

Susan kindly made me a pot of tea and kept me company while I drank it. We discussed what Mrs. Langley had said and agreed she had revealed some interesting and suggestive facts. "For one, Jim Stern is a liar," I said. "He told me he had been turned down as a suitor because he wasn't rich enough for the Langleys. But Mrs. Langley said it was only because he and Elizabeth were too young, and that she and her husband would have consented if he had persevered in his suit."

"Or else Mrs. Langley is a liar," suggested Susan. "It's her word against his, after all. Have you considered that possibility?"

I told her I had, but that I could not reconcile it with Mrs. Langley's thirst for the truth. "If she were involved in her daughter's disappearance, she needn't have done a thing. Chances are they never would have discovered her daughter's body if she hadn't kept agitating in the matter."

"Yes, but calling in a Spiritualist wouldn't be everybody's idea of helping," said Susan shrewdly. "Perhaps she counted on your *not* uncovering the truth. That way she would get credit for trying without risking anything."

I naturally disliked this idea, but there is no use blinking facts, Dear Reader. I have enjoyed a considerable success in discovering lost objects, but invariably these have been objects that I have myself concealed beforehand.

It works in this way. When my agents call on the newly bereaved, they are always on the lookout for small trinkets—nothing so valuable that its disappearance might cause a hue and cry, but rather things with a purely sentimental value. Once I have such objects in hand, I contact the bereaved family, saying their Late Loved One has an urgent message that he or she wishes to communicate from the Other Side.

Not all families respond to these overtures, but many do. If they do respond, I arrange a series of sittings in which the Late Loved One expresses concern over the lost object, urges a search be made, and in general draws the matter out over as long a period as possible. Finally, after the maximum amount of suspense, the Spirit reveals the location where the object may be found—a location, naturally, where I or my agents have previously secreted it. The family regains the valued object; my reputation is enhanced; and everyone ends up happy.

It was possible that Mrs. Langley might have guessed my success in finding lost things was based on some such method. Yet that would mean she had been lying to me from the beginning. I could accept intellectually that this might be the case, but all my instincts assured me otherwise. I told Susan as much, but promised I would be alert to any sign that I might be mistaken.

"In any case, someone is lying about why Mr. Stern was turned down when he offered for Miss Langley. That is suggestive point number one. Number two is the way Miss Langley reacted to her mother's talk about her marital duties—or the way Mrs. Langley said she reacted. Was she frightened away from the whole idea of matrimony? But even if she was, surely she wouldn't have been frightened into committing suicide! I do wish I knew exactly what was said."

Neither Susan nor I had much insight into this matter, since neither of us had had Miss Langley's genteel and sheltered upbringing. Susan, indeed, was skeptical that any woman of eighteen could have been as ignorant of the facts of life as Miss Langley was purported to be.

"It's not reasonable," she argued. "Her mother might think so, but depend upon it she had at least some idea what goes on between men and women. Children see a lot more than their parents give them credit for. Why, I had pieced together the whole business before I was in my teens."

"Very likely," I said. "That is my own feeling as well. But on the other hand, we cannot completely discount the opinions of the people who actually knew Miss Langley. Every one of them has spoken of her—well, call it her unworldliness. Even Miss Stern, who might be considered a hostile witness, said that her parents had kept her in cotton wool. Kept her in the dark, in fact." I shivered. "That was rather horrible, wasn't it? Poor girl, I shall keep thinking about that, I'm afraid: her crying alone in the dark."

Susan said it had given her a queer feeling, too. "But I still misdoubt she was the innocent her parents thought her—at least, by the time she was eighteen. After all, she'd been engaged, or nearly engaged, to two men. She wouldn't have been the first bride to put the marriage bed before the marriage, as the saying goes."

I nodded. "And Jim Stern is the likeliest candidate," I said. "We know that instead of following through on his offer of marriage, he drew back. If he's telling the truth, he did it because her parents rejected him. But if he's lying, as now appears likely, it could be that his relationship with Miss Langley had taken a different turn. Say that they had a physical relationship—a sinful relationship, in Miss Langley's eyes. Perhaps he was blackmailing her on account of it. Or perhaps he merely wanted it to continue and threatened to tell Roland if she broke it off. That would account for everything: her death—by suicide, in this instance—and his concealing her body afterwards out of guilt or fear."

Susan agreed that this theory seemed to fit the facts fairly well.

"The other likely scenario," I continued, "would be if Roland learned of such a relationship and killed her out of jealousy. Or else he killed her simply because she was refusing to marry him. But I don't care much for that theory, because we wouldn't have known she was refusing to marry him if Roland himself hadn't told us. Of course he might just be too dim to realize how it incriminated him. Or perhaps he didn't consider telling a Spiritualist counted!"

Susan smiled and said that was possible. "It's not like talking to the police, at all events," she said. "I'll bet Inspector Harper would like to know what *you* know, after talking to the Sterns yesterday and Mrs. Langley today."

That was when the doorbell rang. We looked at each other. "I'll answer it," she said. "If it's the Inspector, do you want to see him?"

"Yes, very well," I said. My headache was feeling much better after the tea. Besides, I had a bone to pick with Inspector Harper. He had apparently spoken so indiscreetly to Jim Stern that Mr. Stern had rushed straight to me, breathing fiery indignation about my rôle in the affair. I was eager to give the Inspector my opinion of his conduct.

CHAPTER 9

As soon as Susan had ushered Inspector Harper into the Sitting Room, I swept in, giving him a curt nod of greeting. "Good day, Inspector. I am surprised to see you."

"I don't know why you would be," he returned cheerfully. "Last time I was here, I told you I had a presentiment we'd be meeting again over this business."

"Yes, but you also told me I should send for you if I had any further information to share. And I don't recall sending for you!"

"Ah, I had a presentiment about that, too," he said with a nod. "I thought I'd save you the trouble and come around at once."

"Indeed," I said, fixing him with a hard stare. "You somehow divined I have information to share with you? You should set up as a Spiritualist yourself."

"I shouldn't do it half as well as you," he returned equably. "But I do have my sources of information. And when I heard that Jim and Cora Stern had called on you—"

"And how did you hear that?" I demanded.

"As I say, I have my sources of information."

I gave a short laugh. "It would appear the information flows both ways! I was quite surprised to have the Sterns call on me. And I was even more surprised when I learned that you had let slip to Mr. Stern that I was responsible for his being questioned!"

Inspector Harper looked not in the least abashed. Indeed, his eyes were twinkling. "I can't think how I came to do such a thing," he said. "Clumsy of me, wasn't it? You'd think with my experience I'd be more on my guard."

I regarded him for a fulminating moment. "I don't believe it! You deliberately sent him to me? How dare you? I thought Mr. Stern was going to strangle me when I stepped into the room!"

"But he didn't, did he?" The Inspector looked me up and down with a show of anxiety. "You don't appear to have suffered any injury. In fact, you're looking extremely fit. It's not every woman who looks well in black, but you carry it off with a dash."

I wasn't about to be distracted by this kind of cheap flattery. "That is nothing to the point," I said coldly. "Thankfully, Mr. Stern refrained from actually laying hands on me, but he was extremely upset. And indeed, I cannot wonder at it."

"Yes, it's natural enough that he should be upset," agreed the Inspector. "We've been riding him pretty hard, seeing that he seems to have had the best motive for doing away with Miss Langley—or at least for concealing her body, if it happened to be suicide instead. What exactly did he tell you?" he asked. "You didn't happen to make another transcript, by any chance?"

I stared at him, and he stared back at me, his eyes wide and guileless. "Oh, very well," I said, reaching for the bell-pull. "I suppose the sooner you have the information, the sooner you will leave."

He said approvingly that that showed a very sensible attitude. Susan brought him the transcript at my bidding, and I opened up my own pretty writing desk so that he might sit down and copy it in comfort. When he was done, however, he did not immediately take himself off, but leaned back in the desk chair and regarded me with a quizzical expression.

"Well, there's some interesting matter here," he said. "But it doesn't look as though it gets us much forwarder, on the face of it. You asked some good questions; I just wish you'd gotten some better answers. If only there *had* been some woman friend whom Miss Langley had confided in. It doesn't sound as though Miss Stern were one, at any rate! That's a type of witness I hate: eager to talk about herself, but not having any real information to give." He looked at me expectantly. "And what did Mrs. Langley have to say to you? Have you agreed to sit for her again?"

It took me a moment to bring my sagging jaw back from the floor. "You have been watching my house!" I exclaimed. "Oh, that is simply the limit. To have the police spying on me—me, a respectable businesswoman! I have done *nothing* to merit this kind of surveillance."

"Not spying," he protested. "And it's not you and your business we're keeping under surveillance, so much as who's coming to call on you."

"My customers!"

"Clients," he corrected, his face deadpan. "The preferred term is clients."

I glared at him. "Yes, and you are spying on them. And I will soon *have* no clients if this keeps up. To be embroiled in a police affair is bad enough. To be thought an agent of the police is infinitely worse!"

He protested that the spying, such as it was, was very discreet. "No one'll ever know we've got men watching your place, unless they do something to make themselves liable to police notice. And the same goes for you, too. You say you're a respectable businesswoman—well, as long as you stay that, we've no cause to meddle with you."

He gave me a very direct look. "As I said before, I've been making inquiries about you, Madame Fox. You're obviously a very clever

woman. Assuming you do use your Spiritualism to milk your clients—and that's only an assumption, based on my experience with
others in your profession—then you've done it so well, and given
your clients such good value for their money, that not one of them
has a word to say against you. What's more, you only accept clients
who can stand to lose a little—a little—"

"Milk?" I suggested with a thin smile.

"Yes, milk," he said, smiling back at me. "I don't like to see poor
folk defrauded of their livelihoods. I don't like to see those who
haven't enough to begin with, robbed of the little they have. But if
your rich widows and retired colonels want to pay to sit in the dark
and play games with your Spiritograph, I've nothing to say against
it."

For a moment I could not speak. Of course he was exactly right
in his assumptions, Dear Reader. Obviously I had fooled him not at
all. On the other hand, I found myself almost pleased by the masterly
way he had summed up my working philosophy. It is always pleasant
to be understood and appreciated, even if the appreciation comes
from one's natural enemy.

I was struck, too, by his way of expressing himself. Between you
and me, Dear Reader, I am indeed accustomed to think of myself in
a pastoral rôle, although the image I prefer is not that of a milkmaid,
but rather a shepherdess. Spiritualism *is* a religion of sorts, and in
tending my little flock, I am certainly no more venal than many a
man of the cloth. If I were to slaughter one of my lambs (figuratively
speaking), I might profit in the short run, but I could do so only
once. More importantly, I would be likely to draw the unwelcome
attention of the Law, which is apt to obtrude itself when large sums
of money change hands (never mind how I know this).

If, on the other hand, I content myself with merely shearing my
flock on a regular basis, we can all live in Arcadian bliss for years.

The Inspector could not know my thoughts, but he was watching my face. When he spoke again, his voice was coaxing. "As I say, the police have no call to meddle in your business, Madame Fox. You mustn't think I mean to hold that as a club over you. At the same time, if you *would* consider acting for us—not as an agent exactly, but as a sort of unofficial assistant, you'd be very useful to us. A woman in your position sees and hears a lot, and you obviously have sources of information that aren't available to us."

My brows drew together at this. It would be too much if he had uncovered all my little intelligence network. I might as well leave London at once. But before I could speak, he went on in a bland voice. "Spirits, I mean. You have your spirit sources to draw upon."

"Yes, of course," I said flatly. "Spirits."

"So what do you say, Madame Fox? Will you throw in your lot with us?"

I eyed him with resentment. I would have liked very much to reject his proposition out of hand, but only the briefest consideration showed me how imprudent that would be. He might assure me he did not mean to hold a club over me, but such an assurance from the police was meaningless. Obviously he could make life so impossible for me that there would be nothing to do but go back to America (which, in view of my past activities, was probably still too hot for me) or to France (still too hot likewise, plus my French has grown sadly rusty from disuse).

"This is very irregular," I said, stalling for time.

"Indeed it is," he agreed readily enough. "On the other hand, the force has a long-established policy of using informants. We've not used any spiritualists before, but I don't see any reason why we couldn't, assuming you're willing. You've already been extremely useful to us. In fact, not to put too fine a point on it, we'd have got nowhere without you."

This made me feel a little better. I would still have liked to decline his offer, but I could see I had no choice. And he had been very tactful on the whole, putting it in terms that salved my pride and allowing me to maintain the fiction that my private sources of information were Spiritual.

"Very well," I said. "If you think I can do any good, I'm sure I'm . . . *happy* to be of help."

He congratulated me on my civic-minded attitude. "I don't mind telling you, I'll take any help I can get at this point," he added with a sigh. "I've been years—*years*—working on this case, without getting so much as a glimmer of a real lead."

"Chasing after White Slavers and young women on bicycles?" I suggested.

He rolled a humourous eye at me. "You haven't any idea. The newspapers only reported the more *credible* leads. That gives you some notion of what the rest of them were like! We've had every lunatic in Britain writing us with some kind of half-baked theory. Most of the time we knew we were chasing after red herrings, but of course we have to follow up all the leads we get."

I could not help being interested by this insight into police work, which until now I only knew from the other side, as it were. "It must be very tiresome," I said. "At least now you can focus on finding the criminal, rather than proving there was a crime in the first place."

"Yes, and in theory that ought to make it easier. But we're hampered by the fact that it's been three years. The evidence is pretty thin on the ground at this point, and I tend to doubt it was ever very plentiful."

"I suppose not," I said. "You must be wishing now that you had never been assigned to the case."

To my surprise, he denied this and even seemed to be sincere in his denial. "Anyone who's made the rank of detective inspector knows that there must be difficult cases along with the easy ones," he said. "I get my share of both, and very properly, too. And though you may not believe me, I often prefer the difficult ones."

"Indeed," I said. "I would not have supposed that. It seems a peculiar taste!"

"A bit peculiar, perhaps," he agreed, smiling. "But you've got to consider that most day-to-day police work is straightforward enough in all conscience. Low crimes, for low motives—all depressingly simple and sordid. There's a satisfaction in sorting out a really puzzling crime, even apart from the issue of bringing the culprit to justice—which, of course, we don't always manage to do."

"No," I agreed. "I would think it would be depressing, to go through all the work of an investigation and then have nothing to show for it."

"It is, of course. Naturally we always hope to get a conviction. And naturally we always feel it when we don't. But I try to look at it as a separate issue—a quite different thing from the investigation itself. If I've done my work properly, and found out the truth of the matter, and dug up every bit of evidence there is to prove it, then I've succeeded even if the case won't hold up in court. That's the only way to look at it. Otherwise, you'd soon come to the conclusion that the job wasn't worth doing at all."

I could understand this easily enough, Dear Reader. Indeed, though I did not say so to him, it was surprisingly similar to some aspects of my own work. Much of the information I acquire about potential clients I am never able to use at all, owing to some absurd prejudice on their part against Spiritualism. Or they may be like Mrs. Gilbert, preferring simple assurances about their deceased relative's happiness when I am able to supply them with so much more. Or I may make an initial investigation about a new client—much as I did for the Langleys—only to ultimately decide against sitting for them. It is a form of wastage that one simply learns to accept.

Aloud, I contented myself with saying, "That seems a very sensible way of looking at it, Inspector. But do you think you will succeed in discovering the truth about what happened to Elizabeth Langley?"

"God knows," he said frankly. "It's been the very deuce of a case so far. At first sight, there doesn't seem to be but a couple of likely suspects—that's the two young men, of course. They've both got what you'd call decent motives. But there's not a shred of real evidence to tie them to it, seemingly. After that, you've got the father and the servants, which are at least possible, but none of 'em seems to have a motive. And once you get outside them, the field is completely open. It could be anybody, even Miss Stern's tramp!" He tapped the Stern transcript with his forefinger.

"I notice you do not number Mrs. Langley among the suspects," I said.

He shook his head with decision. "Not unless she's mad. And that's not the impression she's given me. No, I think she's exactly what she appears to be: a woman who wants the truth. And she hasn't been the least bit impressed by my efforts to find it out for her." He smiled ruefully. "I expect she said as much when she called on you this afternoon. Have you a transcript for that, too, by-the-by?"

"I haven't had time to make one," I said. "Seeing that you hardly waited until she had left before showing up on the doorstep!"

He apologized so humbly that I relented and told him that I did have some notes on the conversation, although they were still in a rough form. "It would be easiest if I sat down and wrote the whole thing out now, while it's still fresh in my memory," I said. "Do you want to wait, or shall I send it round later?"

He chose to wait, so I took his place at the writing desk and rang Susan to bring the notes from my interview with Mrs. Langley. "And also some tea, please—and some of those cakes you made yesterday, if there are any left."

After a little polite dissembling, the Inspector accepted a cup of tea and a seat on the sofa, where he ate a great many of Susan's excellent cakes while I transcribed her notes into longhand. She does not use shorthand *per se*, but rather a private system of abbreviations and references, with the contents more or less verbatim depending on the pace of the conversation. I always take care to speak clearly and slowly when she is taking notes, but of course my fellow conversationalists are not always so considerate. Mrs. Langley, however, had not challenged Susan's powers unduly. It was all down very much as I remembered it.

As I wrote out the dialogue in my best handwriting, however, I found my breathing growing shallower and shallower—and not merely because my corset was laced down to company standards.

Several times that afternoon, while Mrs. Langley had been talking, I had felt what might be described as a pricking in my thumbs: a sense that I was hearing something significant. Now that I was reading her words rather than simply hearing them, I could see what that something was. There was a common thread running through the whole conversation which I had missed the first time around. I had the sense of holding one end of that thread in my hand, without being entirely sure where the other end led, yet I was sure I had something. I handed the pages to the Inspector, trying not to look as portentous as I felt. I wondered if he would see it, too.

He read through the transcript, frowning, then glanced up at me. "That's odd," he said. "It looks like Stern lied, doesn't it? Saying the Langleys rejected his suit because he wasn't rich enough."

"I don't think he lied," I said.

Inspector Harper went very still, his eyes focused on mine. "Then you think the Langleys are lying?"

I took the transcript he was holding in one hand and picked up the Stern transcript in the other. "I think *one* of the Langleys is lying," I said, shaking both documents at him. "Who actually talked to Jim Stern when he formally proposed for Miss Langley?"

I could see the Inspector's thoughts revolving, trying to catch up with mine. "That would be Mr. Langley," he said.

"And who had the best chance of making sure Mrs. Langley's letter never reached me?"

It took him a moment to get the significance of that, but he did, and pretty quickly, too. "That, too, would probably be Mr. Langley," he said.

"And who told Mrs. Langley that nothing could bring her daughter back, and that probably the culprit couldn't be brought to justice anyway?"

"Mr. Langley," he said. "But—"

"And who sent away Elizabeth Langley's ayah and made her sleep alone in the dark?"

He stared at me. "That? But all that was ages ago. What could that possibly have to do with this business?"

What I said next surprised even me, Dear Reader. Perhaps you may have heard of trance-speaking. I used to practice it years ago: one went into a trance and one's Spirit Guide (it was often a Red Indian guide in my day) would take control and speak through one's own lips. It was like that now, for without any conscious thought I opened my mouth and said, "Old sins cast long shadows."

He stared at me, and I stared back at him. All in an instant everything had become clear to me. I felt the strangest mixture of emotions: triumph on one hand, pity and disgust on the other.

"Oh, no," he said slowly. I could see the revulsion growing on his face as he caught my meaning. "You mean—oh, no."

I nodded. "It would explain everything."

"But—" I could see he was as shaken as I was and even more shocked. "But for him to—to debauch his own daughter! I don't believe it. That is to say, in my police work, among the lower classes—certainly I have encountered cases. But for Charles Langley—a *gentleman*—"

"You English," I said, shaking my head. "You put so much emphasis on birth and position."

This earned me a look of surprise. "But you're English yourself, aren't you?" he said. "You certainly speak like an Englishwoman." Fortunately, he was still too distraught to follow up my slip. "I must say, this is the last thing I would have ever suspected. And if it's true—" he ran a hand through his hair, "if it's true, we'll never be able to make a case. It stands to reason that there won't be any evidence, after all this time."

As he agonized aloud about the difficulty of prosecuting such a case, I watched him with a sense of detachment. The idea of an upper-class father sexually molesting his daughter wasn't quite the shock to me that it was to him. I do not mean that I have any first-hand experience, Dear Reader, for though my own father certainly had his faults, none of them were of *that* magnitude. In my professional capacity, however, I have heard admissions that would curl your hair. The Spirit Parlour sometimes functions as a confessional as well as a theatre.

Eventually the Inspector stopped agonizing and directed a frowning look at me. "I'm still not sure I believe it. It must be all guesswork at this point. Even if, for argument's sake," he drew a deep breath, "even if I were willing to credit that Charles Langley had an incestuous relationship with his daughter, would he murder her as well?"

"If he thought it was going to come out, he might," I said. "Can't you see why? It would be the most dreadful scandal, ten thousand times worse than her simply having a love affair with a boy her own age. I do not insist on murder, however. It's possible that she committed suicide because of it, and he buried her body to cover it up."

"But either way, that doesn't seem quite to explain her behaviour," he said. "If it had happened when she was nine or ten, why would she have waited so long to act?"

I regarded him with a pitying eye. "Because she didn't know any better. How would she? When you're nine or ten, you believe what your parents tell you. And she was such an innocent girl, even into her teens. Everyone we have spoken to stresses that. He probably told her it was a perfectly natural thing, but that decent, well-brought-up girls didn't talk about it."

Inspector Harper's face was wearing a look of revulsion again. "So it was her mother's talk about . . . about her future marital duties that finally opened her eyes?"

"I think it must have been. From what Mrs. Langley said, I have a dreadful feeling that she made a great point of telling her daughter that decent, well-brought-up girls were supposed to be pure in mind and body before marriage. And Mr. Roland, too, has a fixation about purity. I am sure that is why she tried to break her engagement. She realized she wasn't pure, although she was certainly innocent in a sense. Just not in the sense that her future husband would expect."

Again Inspector Harper ran his fingers through his hair. "I don't like this," he said, in what was obviously an understatement. "It's plausible. I admit it's plausible. But it's still all guesswork. How am I going to prove it?"

I couldn't help him there. Indeed, I felt that my part of the work was done. I had found a solution to the mystery, and now it was up to the police to prove it, and to get a conviction if they could. That was their affair, not mine.

I did feel a pang of compunction when I thought of poor Mrs. Langley, however. As bad as it had been for her to find her daughter dead, finding her husband responsible for that death—whether actually or morally—must be immeasurably worse. The attending circumstances made it worse still. She might not even believe it possible.

I couldn't decide if it would be worse if she did, or if she didn't. What I could easily decide was that I wanted nothing more to do with as nasty a business as I had ever been involved in.

So I sat quietly, watching Inspector Harper pace up and down and mutter to himself. Eventually he awoke to the fact that he had been there for most of the afternoon, and that it was almost the dinner hour. "I must go," he said. "I'll have to lay this before the Chief Commissioner[3]—and God knows what he'll say about it. But thank you for your help, and for the tea and cakes." Scooping up both transcripts, he strode toward the front door. Susan was barely in time to open it for him, and he would have forgotten his hat and coat entirely if she had not scurried after him to give them back.

Knowing he was going to lay a distasteful and nearly unprovable theory in front of his superior officer, I found I was sorry for him, too. Of course it was a relief to have the mystery solved. Even if it wasn't what you could call a satisfactory solution, it probably meant that he wouldn't be bothering me much more.

Surprisingly, I found I was a little sorry about that as well. For a policeman, he was really quite a decent sort, and I had enjoyed crossing swords with him—or would have, under different circumstances. Still, I was relieved that from now on, the sad, sordid drama of Elizabeth Langley's life and death was nothing to do with me.

Or so I supposed at the time. But the following day, something happened that caused me to take a much more personal view of the matter.

---

3 The head of the Metropolitan Police is properly termed "Commissioner" alone, but in referring to him as the "Chief" or "Chief Commissioner," Inspector Harper is following contemporary usage. Interested Readers are referred to the correspondence of James Monro and the reports of Detective Inspector Whicher.—*Ed.*

CHAPTER 10

I didn't sleep well that night. Thoughts of Elizabeth Langley, her abominable father, and her anguished mother kept running through my head. It wasn't until a very late hour that I fell at last into a light and troubled slumber.

I awoke late the next morning and was obliged to take a cup of strong coffee before I felt awake even then. Clearly, I needed to take more than coffee; I needed to take myself in hand. It was time to put the Langley affair behind me. I could do nothing more about it, and I didn't want to do anything more about it. All I wanted was for my life to return to its normal, pleasant, orderly routine.

As I toyed with toast and marmalade and drank another cup of coffee, I considered how soon that was likely to happen. I had no idea how the police would proceed from this point. They might hope to learn more from me and my sources, or they might decide (as I already had) that my part was played and they needed me no more.

What I wanted to know most urgently was whether they would continue their surveillance of the Temple of Spiritualism. It had been a shock to learn about that surveillance on the previous day. I have already alluded to my little intelligence network, and to Felicity and the other agents who bring me letters, trinkets, and useful information. The last thing I wanted was to have the police take an interest in their activities.

It wasn't solely on my own account, either. Although my agents work for me, they do not work *only* for me. Many of them engage in multiple lines of business, some of which the police would regard even less sympathetically than, say, the temporary detention of letters from their rightful owners.

It was thus very urgent that I should inform them that my place of business was being watched, and that they should avoid calling on me until further notice. As soon as I finished my toast and coffee, I put on a plain dress and a hat with a heavy veil and slipped out through the side door.

It was a dark day, threatening rain. Before I had gone half a block, the threat was fulfilled, and drops began to patter down around me. They soon settled into a steady, soaking rain that looked as though it meant to keep it up all day. On the whole, I welcomed this circumstance. In a sea of umbrellas, I would be that much less noticeable. I did not think the police surveillance extended to me personally, but I wasn't going to take any chances. Emulating my namesake fox, I darted across streets and through alleys and byways, doubling back on my track several times. Only when I was sure that no hounds of the law were on my trail did I venture to call on my agents.

This took a considerable time. There are a number of people in London who assist me in my business to a greater or lesser degree. In some cases, there was no need to call upon them in person; it was simply a matter of dropping a letter in a post-box, or of placing a discreet advertisement in one of the daily newspapers, to forestall them coming to the Temple on their regular scheduled day.

In other cases, however, the matter was more urgent, and these means would not suffice. In the space of that single afternoon I was obliged to visit a servants' employment agency (in Kensington), a tobacconist's shop (in Soho), the private secretary of a very important gentleman (in Mayfair), two Turkish bathhouses (in the City), a hairdresser's where society women were wont to gossip indiscreetly (in Bloomsbury), and quite a number of other widely scattered locales. What made it worse was that I felt obliged to go for the most part on foot. As anyone knows who reads the published accounts of criminal cases, taking a cab, omnibus, or train puts one at the mercy of people like drivers and conductors, who may then turn around and give information about one's movements to the police.

When I left the tea shop where I had met Felicity—my final call of the day—I was feeling both footsore and fatigued. The rain had stopped, but a heavy fog was rolling up from the river. Despite my fatigue, I hailed it with pleasure. Night was falling fast, and between the dark and the fog I thought I might be able to slip back into the Temple without the police being aware I had ever left it. But it mattered little at this point. They could hardly object to my stepping out for a few hours; it was not as though I were under arrest.

By the time I reached my block of Wimpole Street, the fog had grown so thick that the streetlamp on the corner appeared only as a dim, yellowish glow above my head. The row of shops opposite was completely invisible, concealed by a swirling wall of white. I went along slowly, straining my eyes to see the lamp Susan leaves burning in the Temple's front window.

There is a narrow passage between my own building and the one beside it, leading to a mews behind. I had just passed this alleyway when I heard a rush of footsteps behind me. I had no time to turn and hardly time even to draw breath before I was caught suddenly around the waist, then round the throat, and dragged backward in a crushing embrace.

It happened so fast I had no time to cry out, and once the arm was across my throat I couldn't. My left arm was pinioned to my side, but my right was free, and I tried desperately to pull away the arm around my throat. That effort was futile, but one of my fingers brushed against the head of a hatpin where it skewered my hat to my hair. I had just presence of mind enough to pluck the pin from my head and stab with it—only a feeble stab, under the circumstances, and quite at random. I could not see what I was aiming for; I could only hope I would hit *something*.

Evidently I did, for there was a grunt of pain, and the grip on my throat slackened a bit. I drew a deep breath and then screamed what I believe is popularly called bloody murder.

At almost the same instant, a whistle rang out. My assailant let out a curse, shoved me to the ground, and was away in an instant. I fell onto my hands and knees and remained there, drawing rasping breaths, as a hulking figure emerged from the fog.

"Are you all right, ma'am?" inquired the figure. It proved to be a uniformed police constable, very young and very large, with a rosy face and a pair of bright blue eyes. At that moment, he appeared to me like St. George in brass buttons. Never before have I hailed the sight of a policeman with such pleasure—never, indeed, until that moment.

"Are you all right, ma'am?" he repeated more urgently. I thought he ought to have been able to see I wasn't all right: that I was, on the contrary, gasping like a landed trout. But I suppose there are conventions in these things. "Because if you are," he went on, in a painstaking manner, "I ought to see if I can catch that fellow before he gets too far."

I didn't at all like the idea of being left alone in the fog. "My throat hurts," I said hoarsely. "I would like to get inside."

I could tell he wasn't happy to let my attacker escape without making any attempt at pursuit, but he chivalrously helped me to my feet, picked up my umbrella and other scattered belongings, and walked me to my door. Susan answered the bell, and her eyes went round as saucers when she saw me standing on the doorstep, wet and disheveled and on the arm of a policeman.

"What happened?" she gasped.

My rescuer, introducing himself as Police-Constable Shaw, explained what had happened. "She ought to have a doctor," he added, looking at me with concern.

"No," I croaked. "No doctor." My opinion of doctors is almost as low as my opinion of policemen, Dear Reader—perhaps even lower. Certainly after the experience I had just undergone, P.C. Shaw had done much to redeem the latter profession in my eyes.

In any case, I was pretty sure by now that no serious damage had been done. My throat was sore, and I undoubtedly had a fine assortment of bruises from the neck down, but nothing worse.

P.C. Shaw and Susan were both inclined to argue my decision, but I overruled them. They had to make do with helping me into the Sitting Room and arranging me tenderly on the sofa. I made no objection to this, and when Susan suggested brandy, I made no objection to that, either.

"I'd best get the Inspector," said P.C. Shaw. "He'll want to know about this." Resuming his helmet, which he had politely removed on entering the house, he went back into the fog.

I plucked the remaining hatpins from my hat, tossed it and my veil onto the floor, and leaned back, shutting my eyes. Eventually Susan came back with the brandy. She appeared so much shaken that I invited her to have some as well. The brandy stung a bit going down, but then it usually does. In any case, I definitely felt the better for it.

"Do you think someone was trying to kill you?" asked Susan in an awed voice.

"Yes," I said, gingerly exploring my bruised throat with my fingertips.

"Mr. Langley?" she asked, lowering her voice. Of course she knew all about my epiphany on the previous day.

"I can't think who else it would be," I said. A wave of righteous anger swept over me, or perhaps it was merely the brandy. In any case, I no longer felt shaken, but rather suddenly, aggressively militant. Swinging my legs over the sofa, I sat up and polished off the rest of the brandy at a draught. "How dare he?" I said through my teeth. "How *dare* he?"

At that moment, there were footsteps in the corridor. An instant later, Inspector Harper rushed into the room, followed by P.C. Shaw. I turned a stern eye on them both and demanded to know what they meant by entering my house without knocking or ringing the bell.

"Well, it's easy to see you weren't *too* seriously injured," said Inspector Harper. He came over to where I was sitting, squatted down, and placed a hand on either side of my face, gently turning it from side to side to inspect my throat. "Yes, I see. It could be worse, but you ought to have a doctor nonetheless."

I said mulishly that I wanted no doctor. "I only want to be left alone. This is what comes of having the police meddle in my affairs!"

P.C. Shaw looked shocked, Dear Reader. I don't think he was used to hearing his superior officer addressed in this way. Inspector Harper, however, only said that it was a great shame, but couldn't be helped. "And I must say it makes my job easier, in a way. If it was Langley who did this, we've a good chance of tying him to it—much better than that other business."

It was quite a pleasure to vent my fury on someone. "Oh, I'm so pleased my nearly being murdered makes your job *easier*," I said. "First you spy on me and my business and make me complicit in your vile investigation. And now you're using me like—like a tethered goat to catch a tiger!" (I am a great admirer of Mr. Kipling's Indian stories, Dear Reader.)

Inspector Harper's lips twitched. "I suppose it is rather like that," he said. "But we certainly never intended that you personally should run any risk. That was part of the reason I was having my men keep an eye on your place."

He directed a severe look at P.C. Shaw, who blushed. "It was the fog, sir," he explained. "I was watching all right, but you couldn't hardly see your hand in front of your face. I saw her pass by, and then I heard a scuffling a minute later—and I blew my whistle and rushed right in."

"Yes, he did," I told Inspector Harper. "Don't you go blaming him. He might even have caught Langley if he hadn't had to stop to help me."

Inspector Harper looked bemused and P.C. Shaw gratified by these words. "Very well," said the Inspector, after a moment. "I will admit the fog was a complicating factor." He switched his gaze to me. "As was your being out of the house in it. Didn't you think that might be a bit of a risk, under the circumstances?"

"There wouldn't have been a risk if it weren't for you!" I shot back.

An odd little smile appeared on his lips. "Ah, you're too modest," he said.

I was rather taken aback by this accusation, Dear Reader. Excessive modesty is not a charge with which I am very familiar. Indeed, throughout the course of my life, people have more often hinted that I have an excessively *good* opinion of myself. I mention this so you may know that I am endeavouring to be completely can-did with you, even at my own expense. To the Inspector, however, I merely said that I didn't follow him.

"What I mean is, you're the one who located Elizabeth Langley's body," he explained. "That must have been a nasty shock to her killer."

"To Langley," I said at once.

"Well, we'll say to Langley, for argument's sake. He must have been feeling pretty secure that her body would never be found. But then you find it—you, with the help of your Spiritograph. Of course he's worried about what else you're going to find out."

In fact, Dear Reader, this aspect of the affair had not occurred to me. Being a complete skeptic myself about Spiritualism—at least until the night of the Langley séance—I had not made allowance for how others with less experience might have viewed that night. For all Mr. Langley knew, I might always be able to obtain such results with the Spiritograph.

His attempt to murder me was a little more explainable in this light, but certainly no more justifiable. "I don't need a Spiritograph to tell me he's guilty," I said shortly. "I hope you will lose no time in arresting him."

"You're *sure* it was Langley?" he said.

I was obliged to admit that I had not actually seen my attacker. "But yes, I'm sure it was he. Who else could it have been?"

The Inspector shook his head. "I know you're convinced it was he. Between you and me, I'm convinced you're right. But the Chief didn't think much of your theory when I laid it out for him last night." He winced, as in recollection. "Of course, your being attacked tonight gives it a little more credibility. I'll definitely investigate, and if there's any reasonable evidence, I'll pull Langley in. Can you recall anything that might help to identify him as your attacker?"

I thought about it, and did recall one circumstance that had hitherto slipped my mind. "He should be wounded," I offered. "Where I stabbed him."

The Inspector, Susan, and P.C. Shaw all looked at me. "You *stabbed* him?" asked the Inspector.

"Only with a hatpin," I said regretfully.

"With a hatpin," repeated the Inspector.

"It won't be much more than a pinprick, I'm afraid. It's too much to hope that I hit anything vital. I only wish," I said viciously, "that I had put his eye out."

The Inspector murmured something to P.C. Shaw. I could not hear all of what he said, but thought I could distinguish the word "termagant."

"I suppose it would have been more ladylike of me simply to faint and let him strangle me at his convenience," I said coldly.

"No, not at all," said the Inspector with great politeness. "The wound would be an excellent proof, if it should be somewhere visible."

"But if it's not?"

He hesitated. "It might be difficult if it's not," he said. "As I say, the Chief isn't convinced on the evidence that Langley is responsible. Even if the case against him were stronger than it is, we'd have to proceed cautiously. He's a rich man with considerable influence. We can't just pull him in and search him for a wound. I'll certainly make inquiries, and if we can prove he was in your neighbourhood at the time of the attack, that might be enough. Or if he's got a visible wound."

"I suppose I must be satisfied with that," I said. "Seeing that I myself lack both riches *and* influence."

"Oh, I say, ma'am," said P.C. Shaw, looking shocked once more. I think he would have made some further protest, but the Inspector shook his head at him.

"You may be sure we will do our very best, Madame Fox," he said. "And just in case, I'll make inquiries about the young men, too. They're out of it if your theory is right, but it won't hurt to make sure." He shot me a glimmer of a smile. "After all, you said you were afraid Jim Stern was going to strangle you the first time you met him!"

Swinging into action, he scribbled half a dozen messages on his notepad and dispatched them via P.C. Shaw to the nearest police station. For the next few hours, there was a constant stream of policemen in and out of the Temple. Around midnight, the Inspector himself departed, but he left P.C. Shaw behind, just in case (he said) Langley should attempt another murderous attack. Of course I protested at having a policeman billeted upon me, but between you and me, Dear Reader, both Susan and I slept the better for knowing P.C. Shaw was posted in the corridor downstairs, a most substantial barrier to any potential evildoer.

CHAPTER 11

On the following day, the Inspector called to let me know the results of his investigation.

Those results were rather mixed, Dear Reader. The good news was that Charles Langley was proved to have been in London the previous evening and within walking distance of the Temple. "He arrived in Town around mid-day and stayed at his club last night," Inspector Harper told me. "And he could easily cover the distance between here and there on foot. It's only a matter of some ten or twelve blocks."

The bad news was that he seemed to have an alibi. "He had an early dinner, and the porter swears he never set foot outside afterwards." The Inspector drove his fingers through his hair in his habitual gesture of frustration. "That porter! The man's a fool—nothing more nor less. I've seen the little cubbyhole where he sits. There's a half-door with a window above it that looks into the front hall, so he can keep an eye on anyone coming or going. That's the theory, anyway. But you can't see the front door without standing up and coming right over to the window. And he's got an easy chair in the corner with a stack of sporting papers and a spirit lamp to make tea. You can't tell me someone couldn't slip in and out without his noticing, if they chose their moment and were careful to do it quietly."

The Inspector smacked one hand against the other. "I charged him with it—pointed out that he must have taken his eyes off the door if he sat down at all. But nothing I could say would make him admit it. He swears Langley never went out, and that's that."

I considered this for a moment or two. "Langley's clothing should have been wet," I said. "The fog was very heavy. And he had to use both hands when he attacked me, so he wouldn't have been holding an umbrella."

"Unfortunately, the porter says he was out earlier that afternoon, when it was still raining," said the Inspector. "He had made a note of it in his book and showed it to me with great triumph—as if it proved Langley couldn't have gone out again later! Of course it does nothing of the sort. But unfortunately it does give a legitimate reason for Langley's clothing to be wet. Which it was—we've got the statement of another of the club servants to prove it."

Matters thus appeared to be at an impasse. I said as much, and the Inspector admitted it, but said the circumstance of my being attacked gave him at least some leeway for action. "We already have a watch on your place. I'll keep my men on it for the time being, as well as having Shaw stay with you nights. Meanwhile, I'll keep working to try to get some evidence against Langley. Perhaps he was reckless enough to take a cab. Or perhaps someone saw him between here and his club, even in spite of the fog. It's at least a possibility."

I suggested the Inspector might make inquiries of my neighbours on either side, or of the other tenants in the building, in case one of them had seen or heard something. "Langley couldn't have known I would come home at that particular time," I said. "For I didn't know it myself. It was purely a matter of happenstance. It stands to reason he must have been loitering in the alleyway some little time, on the chance I might go in or come out."

The Inspector nodded. "Yes, we thought of that. So far we've had no luck turning up anyone who saw him there, but you never know." He paused, eyeing me rather speculatively. "Of course your side door opens into the alley," he said. "So he could watch both it and the front door if he stationed himself near the alley entrance. It's the logical place to choose for that purpose, and it's got the added advantage of being inconspicuous. I wonder, though—you're sure he didn't have any means of knowing your movements beforehand? You hadn't made any appointment he might have caught wind of?"

"No, indeed," I said. I had made no appointments with Felicity and her compatriots, and the idea that Charles Langley might have learned anything from them would have been laughable in any case. There could be no two castes in London less likely to exchange confidences.

"Then it seems to me unlikely his first plan was to attack you in the street," said the Inspector, still contemplating me with a speculative air. "If what you say is true, it would have been a long chance to catch you outside at that particular time. On the whole, I have to wonder if he wasn't in the alley looking for a way to force an entrance into your place—through your side door, perhaps, or one of the windows."

This was a very unwelcome thought. My expression must have shown how unwelcome it was, for the Inspector looked at me curiously. "You didn't think of that?" he asked.

"No, I naturally concluded murder was his goal when I felt his arm across my throat."

"And so it may have been. But if a man sets out to commit murder in cold blood, he would be a fool to do it in the street when he might do it with much greater safety and privacy indoors—someplace where he would be away from prying eyes and possible interference.

It's only you and your housekeeper who sleep here on the premises, isn't it?"

"Yes," I said, misliking the trend of the conversation more and more.

"And Langley probably knew that, or at least guessed it. You don't keep a carriage?"

I shook my head, feeling more and more dismayed as I followed the line of the Inspector's reasoning. "No, I don't. And Langley would have known it, for when I went to his home to meet with him and his wife the first time, I went in a cab. Since I didn't come in my own carriage, he would have been able to guess that I didn't have one. And from that, he would have been able to guess that I had no coachman or groom." I looked at the Inspector unhappily. "And when he came here for the séance, Susan opened the door to him and took his coat and hat. She is the only servant he would have seen. So, yes, he might easily have guessed it would only be Susan and I here nights, with no manservant about."

The Inspector's face was somber. "There you are. No menservants, nothing but women in the house. He might have concluded it would be easy enough to break in, and then commit whatever crime he had in mind. Mind you, it might have been nothing worse than smashing up your Spiritograph," he finished, with an attempt at levity.

"But you don't believe that," I said.

He looked at me, his face unwontedly grave. "No, I don't. And the reason I don't is because he tried to strangle you, there in the alley. He needn't have done that, if he was just lurking there to force an entrance later on, in order to burgle, or vandalize, or commit some other crime against property. Your passing by when you did might have been just chance, but the way he reacted shows the way his mind was working."

"Toward murder," I said. I pondered this a little while. "If he tried to murder me, don't you think that proves he murdered his daughter?" I asked.

"Yes, I do," he said at once. "And probably he murdered her in the same way. That's another thing we learn in the force. Murder is a crime anyone can commit, but those who commit it more than once tend to stick to the same method over and over again. Strangulation has a lot of advantages, too, as far as it goes. It's relatively quick, and it's quiet enough if you catch the victim when she isn't expecting it—and when she isn't armed with a hatpin," he added, with a flash of a smile. "It takes no special equipment, no weapon that might be discovered on your person later, like a knife or bludgeon. It leaves nothing which might be stained with the victim's blood to tell the tale—no blood on the weapon, and none on the murderer's clothing."

"If he did strangle her, might that explain why the doctors couldn't tell if she were murdered?"

"Yes, it might. Generally, strangulation leaves marks on the soft tissues—as you know." His eyes rested upon my neck. I was wearing a dress with a high collar to hide the bruises, Dear Reader, but with only partial success. It would be a while before I cared to appear in full evening décolletage again. "But unless it's done with terrific force, strangulation typically doesn't damage the underlying skeleton. When we found poor Miss Langley, she had been dead so long there weren't any soft tissues left."

The Inspector let me digest this, too, for a while before he spoke again. "I don't wish to alarm you, Madame Fox, but I would urge you and your housekeeper to take every possible care while we are making our investigation. Keep your doors and windows shut and locked, especially at night. Don't let anyone in whom you don't recognize. As I say, I have my men watching the place, and Shaw will stand guard here nights, but you can't be too careful. Keep that hat-pin by you at all times, too," he added, smiling.

"I'll take care I have a more effective weapon than that," I said.

I meant it quite literally, Dear Reader, but I think he thought I was joking, for he reached in his pocket and drew out a policeman's whistle, saying that if Susan or I needed assistance, a whistle would bring one of his men around straightaway.

"By-the-by," he added, as he was preparing to leave, "I did check on Giles Roland and Jim Stern as well. They both have alibis of a sort, though neither is what you'd call conclusive. Roland was at home all evening, but his is a small bachelor establishment, and his manservant had the day off. He keeps a couple of maidservants who saw him intermittently throughout the afternoon and evening, but if he had wanted to, I think he could have slipped out of the house for a couple of hours without their knowing it."

"I don't believe it was Roland," I said decidedly. "He is hardly taller than I am. It was a bigger, stronger man who attacked me."

The Inspector accepted this, though he warned me that assumptions about strength based on size could be deceptive. "As for Stern, he was dining in Town last night—just a quiet dinner with a few friends. They can vouch for him during the time they were together, but the dinner didn't start until eight o'clock or thereabouts, and he drove himself into Town with no groom. So he might have made a detour beforehand to come by your place, though I think the times are too tight to make that likely."

"It's not likely in any case," I said. "All this is admirable police work, Inspector, but I am positive Charles Langley is your man."

"Well, let us hope I can make the Chief think so, too," he said with a sigh. "And then convince a jury as well. For that, it's es-sential—*essential*—that we prove Charles Langley was able to leave his club without the porter seeing him." Squaring his shoulders, he left the house, vowing that he would shake the porter's story if it was the last thing he did.

I could not feel very hopeful, Dear Reader. Given my experience with Human Nature, I thought he was not making enough allowance for True Belief.

As you may or may not know, we humans have a natural tendency toward belief. In great matters and in small, consciously and unconsciously, we make our observations about the world and formulate theories to explain them. Once we have settled on a particular belief, we are tenacious in clinging to it. Evidence that conflicts with our beliefs we are likely to reject, no matter how convincing. Evidence that supports our beliefs we triumphantly embrace, no matter how dubious.

I have seen the most striking evidences of this during my career as a Spiritualist. At one séance years ago, I incorrectly named my client's deceased husband George rather than John, owing to an unfortunate lapse in my intelligence network. When the client drew this to my attention, I told her with authority that George was her husband's name in the Spirit World—and she believed me, Dear Reader! Not only that, but during subsequent séances she made a point of addressing him as George, apologizing humbly whenever she forgot and called him John. You will own it was an amazing example of the power of Belief.

I can offer other examples just as amazing. You may remember my mentioning a séance years ago where a gentleman of the press caught me *in flagrante delicto*. Now you would think that the sight of me outside my cabinet draped in phosphorescent muslin and clutching a tambourine would be enough to convince anyone I was a fraud, and among the thinking members of the audience it was. But the True Believers were not shaken for a moment.

They argued that I was entranced at the time, in a state resembling sleep, so that my perambulations with the tambourine were simply a sort of Spiritualistic sleep-walking. Some of them even argued that my physical body was *inside the cabinet all along*, and that what the gentleman of the press actually tackled was my Spiritual emanation. When he tackled it, of course my physical body was instantly freed from its earthly bonds and transported to join with the spiritual, thus explaining my presence outside the cabinet and my absence within it. With these and similar theories did these good people affirm their belief in my Spiritualistic abilities, and in the very teeth of the evidence.

Thus, I was not hopeful that the porter would recant his beliefs any time soon. He might well believe he had never taken his eyes from the door, and that Charles Langley could not possibly have left and returned without his noticing. And of course, if he felt he might be accused of negligence in his job, his belief would be twice as strong, being reinforced by his own self-interest. In any case, it sounded as if the man was stupid as well as stubborn, and there is no doing anything with people of that sort. The two qualities, I have often observed, fuse together into a kind of hard seamless shell that makes their possessor impervious alike to reason and logic. There is no lever that can be used to move him (or her), and nowhere to insert one if there were.

That being the case, I feared Charles Langley was unlikely to be brought to justice anytime soon. In my own mind I had absolutely no doubt of his guilt. I remembered his defensive attitude that first day at the Arbours, the antagonism he had shown me, and the way he had been subtly trying to discourage the investigation all along. I remembered his shuddering sobs after the séance. I had initially taken them at face value as a sign of a father's grief, but I was now convinced they were sobs of guilt and fear that his sins were finding him out. Clearly they were not sobs of contrition, for he had added to his sins since that night, first by waylaying his wife's letter to me, and then by his murderous attack the other night. To me, this proved that he would not stick at murder and that his daughter's death was likewise murder. He had murdered his daughter, and now he had tried to murder me, and it didn't appear the police were going to be able to do anything about it.

I found this completely unacceptable.

There was some comfort in the thought that he was unlikely to make another murderous attack anytime soon. The Inspector warned me that though his officers had been very discreet in their inquiries, Langley would undoubtedly be on his guard from now on if he were indeed the guilty party. Still, as long as he remained at large, I could never be wholly free of the prospect of another attack. I could not decide whether this or the prospect of continued police surveillance were more aggravating. In any case, the two in combination were insupportable.

Susan agreed with me, though she observed that having P.C. Shaw in the house nights had not been as bad as either of us had feared. He was certainly much too large to be decorative, and his enormous boots posed a constant threat to my rugs and furniture. On the positive side, however, he was quiet, respectful, and full of innocent admiration for the Temple's exotic décor. What was more, he was always ready to lend a hand with any household task that called for more brute strength than either Susan or I possessed. We were both inclined to make a pet of him, though he would have been an expensive pet to keep, Dear Reader. The first night she gave him supper in the kitchen, Susan reported that he had eaten a whole cottage loaf and the entirety of the roast joint left over from dinner.

On the whole, I felt the situation was untenable, with or without the prospect of keeping P.C. Shaw with us. I couldn't pursue my usual livelihood inside the Temple owing to the presence of the police. I couldn't go outside without putting my life at risk. Even if I didn't go outside, I could not feel secure, thanks to the Inspector's theory that Langley had been trying to force his way into the Temple that night in the alley.

My rooms had always seemed safe before, but against the prospect of a murderous attack, I wanted something more than ordinary door and window fastenings between me and Charles Langley. There was some comfort in having P.C. Shaw stand guard at night—but that brought us full circle, back to the impossibility of holding any séances while there were police in the house.

It was a situation to chafe even the meekest spirit, Dear Reader. Since my spirit has never been particularly meek, I was more than chafed; I was angry clear through. The fury I had felt lying on the sofa after Langley's attack had not receded as my bruises faded. If anything, it had increased.

It added a very personal element to my feeling against the man. Before the attack, I had despised him heartily and wished the police luck in bringing him to justice, but I had not been tempted to take any hand in the business myself. It was the police's rightful task, I felt, and the reason we pay rates and taxes. But now Charles Langley had meddled with *me*.

This, too, is Human Nature, Dear Reader. Until Self is involved, we may see a wrong or injustice, and even admit it as such, yet feel no compulsion to remedy it. Now, as the days went by, and the Inspector confessed himself no nearer to proving Charles Langley guilty of his crimes, I began to realize that he might never do so. He was hampered by regulations and conventions and notions of justice and fair play that effectively tied his hands. But I was not. I was a free agent, and the Inspector himself had pointed out that I had sources of information that he did not. He was pleased to call them Spirit Sources, but we both knew—or suspected, at least, in his case—that they were human, and that I used them for morally dubious purposes. If I wished, however, I could use them now to bring Charles Langley to justice.

The sticking point, of course, was money. It went strongly against my principles to lay out money that was unlikely to give me any tangible return on my investment. I could not count on receiving any reward from the Langleys, considering that I was doing my best to get one of them hanged. In any case, I was quite sure that Charles Langley would never pay me a penny if left to himself. Mrs. Langley had spoken as if the initial reward for finding her daughter was already as good as mine, but I had not received it yet, and such are the laws regarding marriage and property in England that she might be powerless to pay it herself if her husband baulked. She might not even want to, considering that I would be earning it by depriving her of her husband as well as her daughter.

It was a solemn moment, therefore, when I told Susan I was resolved to undertake the necessary expense. She applauded my decision, which was cheering, although I pointed out it was easy enough for her to approve. *She* would not be the one out-of-pocket by it.

"Ah, well: it shows a nice civic-minded attitude, just like the Inspector says," she returned. She was fond of quoting him at me, Dear Reader; I think it entertained her to hear me bested in argument now and then.

I told her I was not civic-minded at all, just tired of being a prisoner in my own Temple with P.C. Shaw eating me out of house and home. "Langley was lucky the other night, with the fog and the porter," I said. "Even with all their resources, the police haven't been able to prove he attacked me. I doubt we shall be able to, either. To my mind, his crimes against his daughter are his more likely Achilles' heel."

"You mean his murdering her?"

"Yes, and his molesting her, too."

"But all that was a long time ago," said Susan dubiously.

"It is, of course. And we know that the police have investigated at least one of those crimes—his daughter's murder—without finding anything to prove him responsible. But I have been thinking, Susan. Who would be most likely to know if something criminal was happening in the house?"

"The servants," said Susan at once. This is an article of faith with both of us, Dear Reader, and our faith has been borne out by the event, time and time again.

"Precisely: the servants," I said. "Of course the police have spoken with Langley's servants, not once but many times. And they have learned nothing, or at least nothing worth mentioning. But they are hampered in their methods."

"They can't use bribery," said Susan, nodding.

"True," I said, conceding what was certainly a valid point. "But bribery is not exactly what I am thinking about, or at least not by itself. We have another, even more important advantage than being able to use bribery, and that is the advantage of being *unofficial*. As we both know, many people are afraid to talk to the police, even when they are completely innocent of wrong-doing. That is especially true of servants, and for good reason. They have much to lose, and little to gain, especially when they're being asked to testify against the so-called upper classes. And when it's their own employers we're talking about—well, who can blame them if they aren't eager to risk their jobs?"

Susan nodded sagely. "You can't tell me somebody didn't see or hear something. In a great house like that, it's practically a certainty."

She has worked in a great house or two in her time, Dear Reader, so she ought to know. I highly value her experience in these matters.

"Who do you think would be the most likely to have seen or heard something?" I asked her. "Langley's valet?"

Susan considered this with her head on one side. "Maybe. He'd be likely to know Langley's movements on any given day. And if Langley killed his daughter and buried her body, there might have been some sign of it on his clothes—blood, or mud, or something of the sort. Still, that was a long time ago. It's asking a lot to remember back three years."

"Yes, unfortunately it is," I agreed. "And even more unfortunately, it's safe to assume that the police have already questioned the valet about it, and he has denied remembering anything suggestive or significant. What I wondered was whether *we* might be more successful, given our advantage of being unofficial."

Susan did not think we had much advantage in this particular case. "Upper servants are a touchy lot," she said. "I wouldn't pin your hopes on getting anything out of Langley's valet, unless he happened to have a grudge against his master."

"Well, we'll hope he does. We can at least inquire." In imitation of Inspector Harper, I had got my own little notebook, in which I made a note about the valet. "Who else? Butler, housekeeper, cook?"

Susan did not think any of these suggestions very likely, either. "Same trouble," she said. "They're all upper servants, and if they had anything against Langley, the police would have likely got it out of them already. If they don't have anything against him, they aren't likely to betray him now. Not as likely as an underservant, at any rate."

"So you suggest we concentrate on the underservants?"

"Yes, and I'd start with the gardeners. Langley had to use something to bury his daughter, after all. They might have seen him mucking about with their tools, or at least noticed a shovel was missing or something."

I agreed it might be worth following up this idea, though I pointed out that a missing shovel wouldn't be enough evidence to tie Langley to the murder of his daughter. "We can but try, however. What about his other crime? Might someone have known or suspected he was molesting his daughter? We can't talk to the ayah, of course, since she was sent back to India. But it sounds as though he didn't start molesting his daughter until after the ayah left. I had thought of the governess, but she doesn't sound very likely, given what the Sterns told me about her."

"Governesses are no good," said Susan at once. "You can take it from me. A sorry lot they are in general, full of airs and graces and yet not paid what a decent cook makes. You won't learn anything worth knowing from one of them. Anyone who thinks being called a lady is more important than being paid a decent salary has her thinking skewed to start with."

That is certainly my own feeling, Dear Reader, although I felt Susan might possibly be prejudiced in the matter. Still, what I had heard about Miss Pring did not attract me. I put her name beside that of Langley's valet, together with a question mark.

Susan, meanwhile, had been thinking deeply. "The nursery maid," she said suddenly.

"Nursery maid?" I repeated. "Isn't that what the ayah was?"

"No, an ayah's more like a nanny. That's to say, she's the one who's in charge of the nursery. But in such a big household, there would have also been a nursery maid to wait on her, and very likely more than one. But certainly at least one maid, and she would have stayed on after the ayah left. You couldn't expect the governess to lay the fires and make the beds," said Susan with a sniff.

"Make the beds," I repeated.

We looked at each other. "Yes," she said. "Yes, indeed. Put the nursery maid down, by all means. *And* the laundress. When she washed the bed-linens, she might have noticed something."

I felt a tingle of something like excitement as I wrote these suggestions down, Dear Reader. Questioning the valet and the gardeners were obvious lines that the police would have followed, and I had scant hopes of learning anything new by following them myself. But there was just a chance that by consulting the nursery maid and laundress, we might discover something the police hadn't.

"It makes sense," I told Susan. "Because in fact we are investigating an entirely different crime. The police are concentrating on the murder, because to them, there's no real evidence that another crime was ever committed."

Susan agreed. "And it'd be the lesser crime, too, at least to their way of thinking."

"That is right, but though it may be an older, lesser crime, it is also the *pivotal* crime. I'm sure of it. 'Old sins cast long shadows.' And perhaps they are long enough in this case to expose Charles Langley as the villain he is."

CHAPTER 12

Although I had decided to damn expense in the interests of Truth and Justice, Dear Reader, I wanted value for my hard-earned pounds and pence. "Value" in this case meant information, and I wanted it even if it had to be obtained in a manner that did not accord with the Law's niceties.

That meant I wanted Felicity.

I am capable of making my own inquiries, Dear Reader. When it comes to drawing confidences out of dowager countesses and retired colonels, I can hold my own with anybody.

But servants are a different matter. They pose their own set of challenges, not all of which I am equipped to handle. And domestic servants in a big country estate like the Arbours are in some ways the most challenging of all. It wouldn't only be a matter of getting them to talk, but of getting access to them in the first place. Unlike the police, I couldn't simply show up at the door and demand to talk to them.

That is where Felicity comes in. She has a dozen ways of insinuating herself into wealthy households, sometimes for purposes that you and I are probably better off not knowing, Dear Reader. One of her most successful dodges is to go about as a seller of beads, ribbons, beauty aids, and other cheapjack merchandise. Serving women like pretty things as much as their mistresses do, and once Felicity has shown them her wares, she is also in a position to extract information from them.

This can be done using out-and-out bribery, of course. But in fact sympathy can be an even more valuable currency. Felicity is a warm, motherly sort of woman to whom it is natural to tell your troubles. These poor girls in service—many of them just up from the country and away from their families for the first time—often do find themselves in trouble, and sometimes trouble of the most desperate kind. Felicity can assist them in a variety of safe, effective, and (above all) discreet ways. In the case of lesser problems, she can simply lend a sympathetic ear, pat their hands, and encourage them to tell her all about their lives, their loves, and their employers.

And in this way, she learns secrets. I derive much of my own income from the information Felicity provides for me. In a case like this, she was the obvious choice to penetrate into the Langley household in search of something that would incriminate Charles Langley.

I faced a little difficulty at the outset, however. With the police watching my door, I could not ask Felicity to call on me. On occasion we correspond through the mail, or through cryptic notices inserted in the newspapers, but this was too delicate and critical a matter to communicate in any way other than in person. Accordingly, I steeled myself to face the streets of London again, along with the possibility of another attack. I took some obvious precautions, however. Charles Langley would not catch me off guard a second time.

First I donned a mantelet with a high boned collar, into which I had inserted carpet tacks with the points facing outward. No one could grab my throat without immediate and painful consequences. Next, I put the policeman's whistle that Inspector Harper had given me into my pocket. And finally I carried a large sable muff, to conceal the fact that I was also carrying one of Mr. Samuel Colt's fine revolvers, a souvenir of my last, eventful American tour. I was a little uncertain about the legality of my owning and carrying this weapon, for the British traditionally have more conservative views about firearms than Americans do. But I felt I would rather defend my use of the revolver afterwards, if I needed it, than need it and be without it.

Happily, I encountered no difficulties *en route* to my rendezvous with Felicity. This took place once again at a tea-shop, the Calico Cat. The Cat is not so elegant an establishment as one of London's grand hotel tea-rooms, but it is a cozy place, low of ceiling, dim of lighting, and with little tables and calico-upholstered chairs set in nooks that accord a pleasant privacy. I have reason to think Felicity owns a controlling interest in the place. At any rate, she can usually be found there around the hour of five o'clock, indulging in scones, clotted cream, and strong sweet tea.

Having pushed open the shop door and stood a moment to let my eyes adjust to the gloom, I saw with relief that Felicity was present. She is a sweet-faced woman about my own age, as comfortably upholstered as the tea-shop's little chairs. These points of her appearance are more or less unvarying, but everything else about her is subject to the wildest fluctuations. Today she was sporting a front of blonde curls and dressed in a flamboyant fashion: green-and-yellow striped dress, a red fur boa, and a monumental hat crowned with a whole aviary of stuffed birds.

"My dear Seraphina!" she exclaimed, motioning me to the chair opposite her.

"My dear Felicity," I returned, accepting the chair and placing my loaded muff with great care on the empty seat beside me.

"It is a pleasure to see you again," she said, as she beckoned to the attendant. "The scones are fresh, and I can recommend the tea-cakes also. Will you take China or India, Seraphina?"

Once the order was given, and the attendant had gone off to prepare it, we both leaned forward until the brims of our hats touched. "Are the police still watching your place?" she hissed.

"Yes, unfortunately they are," I said. "In a way, that's what I've come about. "

I told her the whole story: about the Langley séance, the discovery of Elizabeth Langley's body, the conclusions I had drawn about Charles Langley's guilt, and the inability of the police to prove those conclusions. I finished by describing the attack upon me, and how even there the police had failed to find any evidence. Felicity listened with rapt attention. She is a wonderful listener, as you might expect, Dear Reader. I felt much better after unburdening myself to her.

"And you want me to . . .?"

"Succeed where the police have failed."

Felicity found this very amusing. "It's a new start to be on the same side as the Law," she remarked. "At this rate, we'll all end up police informers before we're done!" But she sobered quickly as I described the kind of evidence I was hoping to get.

"The nursery maid," she said, nodding with decision. "I'm of the same mind as you, Seraphina. She's the most likely source, and the most likely to pay out quickly."

"Do you think it's worth trying the governess, too?"

Felicity thought not, and in emphatic terms. In fact, she was as derogatory on the whole subject of governesses as Susan had been. "I'll try if you like, dear, but don't get your hopes up," she warned me. "That's a long shot on the outside, whichever way you look at it."

"And the valet?"

"I can try for the valet, too, but that'll take time. Upper servants are a chancy business anyway, unless they've got a grievance. The higher they get, the more they get to believing in the system that set them up, and the less likely they are to peach on their masters and mistresses."

"And the laundress?"

"Ah, I'm afraid there's nothing doing there, dear. I'm not perfectly sure, but I think the Langleys have their laundry work done outside. They live close enough to London to use one of the big professional companies, worse luck."

I did not dream of questioning her sources of information, Dear Reader. Probably the domestic arrangements of every well-off family in Britain are an open book to her. I merely opined that if the trend toward mechanization kept up, servants soon wouldn't exist at all, and there would go our livelihoods.

Felicity agreed it was a shame and a scandal. "But I'll do what I can for you with the Langleys," she said. "Not a household I'm familiar with, but I daresay I can find a way in." She shot me a calculating look. "How much is it worth to you?"

I shut my eyes and took a deep breath. "*Carte blanche,*" I said. "I give you *carte blanche.*" It hurt to think of my hard-earned money going the wrong direction, but business had been good lately, and I supposed I could afford it.

Felicity opened her eyes at this. "What, just to help the police?" she exclaimed.

"Yes—no—not exactly. The man tried to kill me, after all. And he did kill his daughter, after first raping the poor girl—and when she was only a child, too. I look upon it as a public service."

Felicity still looked a bit skeptical, but said it did sound as if the man were a right bastard. I apologize for this vulgarity, Dear Reader, but Felicity has a forthright way of speaking—on occasion, at least. On other occasions, she can sound as refined and genteel as the Queen herself. It would take the pen of Mr. Dickens to capture the complexities of her character.

Having reached an agreement, Felicity and I each had another cup of tea and a nice conversation about other matters of mutual interest. About dusk I took leave of her, after first tickling the ears of the tea-shop's eponymous cat, which lay purring in front of the fire. Some people believe calico cats are lucky, Dear Reader. Perhaps they are, for I arrived safely back at the Temple without any need of collar, whistle, or revolver.

CHAPTER 13

A few days followed, in which I strove to be patient while waiting to hear from Felicity. Her first bulletin was not encouraging. She had made some advances toward the valet and been flatly rejected at every turn:

> *I think he knows something, Seraphina—or suspects it, leastways. But he won't talk to me, nor to any of the other People I've sent to try him, not even to take our money and Lie to us. I fear Someone has got there before us and stop'd his mouth, I know not whether with Threats or Money, but at any rate he is standing Mum and like to stay that way.*

I was sorry to hear it, but after all it was no more than we had expected. The valet had always been an outside chance. Sighing, I went on to Felicity's next paragraph:

> *It is a Queer household altogether, the Servants keeping very much to themselves and not dispos'd to talk to Outsiders, which is to my cost as I doubt not but a couple of the Maids could tell me Something if they would. But never fear, My Dear, for I've another dodge or two yet to try.*

If Felicity thought the maids were concealing Something, then she was probably right. I would trust her instincts as soon as my own in these matters. I went on reading:

> *As regards the Governess, she has been pension'd off and lives now in Clerkenwell not so very far from your Place of Business, My Dear. But she is an Old Fool who gives herself no end of airs and has naught at all to say, at least to such as I. You might have a try at her Yourself if you thought it worth your while, but I doubt whether it is.*

Probably Felicity's instincts were right here, too. Still, I filed the idea away for future consideration, along with the address of Miss Pring's lodging house.

Felicity concluded on a more hopeful note:

> *The Nursery Maid still seems a good Wheeze. She has been let go, I find, but I've a line on her and hope soon to turn up Trumps. Yrs., F.*

In the days that followed I tried to be hopeful about Felicity's search for the nursery maid, for there was little else to feel hopeful about. Inspector Harper called each day to report a continued lack of police progress; P.C. Shaw showed up each night to stand guard and to empty the contents of my larder.

After a particularly maddening day, in which I broke a tea-cup, accused Susan of misplacing my watch (in error, as it turned out), was presented with a butcher's bill of truly staggering proportions, and had my doorbell rung three times by people seeking the dentist next door, I decided I needed to get away from the Temple for a few hours, even at the risk of a possible attack.

"I'll go see the governess," I told Susan. "Perhaps I will be more successful in getting something out of her than Felicity. Even if I am not, it will at least make a change from sitting here and fretting."

Eager as I was to try my luck with Miss Pring, I nonetheless planned my approach carefully. I had the advantage of Felicity's experience to profit by, as well as what I had learned from the Sterns and Mrs. Langley. All of them had stressed Miss Pring's bent for propriety. That being the case, it would not do to appear in my own character as a Spiritualist. There are, of course, many persons of undoubted propriety who patronize Spiritualists (including the Queen herself, as I understand), but there are also many who condemn dealings with the Spirit World and cling to a more orthodox creed. From everything I had heard of Miss Pring, I guessed she would be among this latter group.

For a while I played with the idea of calling on her as a church-woman collecting subscriptions for charity. This is one of the ways my agents use to approach prospective clients. But it has been my experience that asking for money puts one at a disadvantage, even when the money is alleged to be for a worthy cause. Some persons deal very curtly with this kind of caller, Dear Reader. If Miss Pring were living on the pension of a retired governess, she might well be one of them.

On the whole, I thought it might be better to show up seeking information rather than money. People are generally far less stingy with this commodity, assuming they are approached in the proper way. Besides, if by some chance Inspector Harper found out about it, I thought I would rather not have to justify extorting money for a false cause. It was a new thing to find myself so scrupulous on such a point, Dear Reader. There is no doubt but that consorting with the police puts a damper on some of one's more imaginative flights.

There are many guises under which one may go door-to-door obtaining information. For a time, I considered putting on my tailor-made suit and spectacles and appearing as a lady journalist. I feared, however, lest Miss Pring might not approve of lady journalists, who are, after all, an innovation of recent date. Besides, Felicity had spoken of her putting on airs. That hinted at social aspirations, and journalists are very low on the social scale.

In the end, I decided I would be an author rather than a journalist. Even ladies of high degree are known to pursue the avocation of author. Under the pretext of collecting material for a book, I thought I had a decent chance of inveigling the information I wanted from Miss Pring. I planned to stress that it was not a novel I was writing (novels are often frowned on by strait-laced ladies), but rather a scholarly work on education. This had the right ring to it, I felt. In consulting Miss Pring, retired governess, for my scholarly study, I would be conveying a subtle compliment that I hoped would at least get me through the door.

Of course my appearance would be instrumental in achieving this, too. It should hint at wealth and social position without overstepping the line into vulgarity and ostentation. Once more I had recourse to my best black silk dress, the one I had put on to impress Inspector Harper at our first meeting. Accompanied by a hat of irreproachable smartness, both Susan and I felt it struck exactly the right note. Tucking the address Felicity had given me into my pocket, I stepped outside and paused on the doorstep, looking up and down the street.

It was early afternoon, the sun visible as a bright spot in a sky dulled by London's perpetual haze. As usual at that hour, there was a fair amount of traffic in the street, both on foot and in carriage. There were also a few loiterers hanging about the apothecary's opposite. It all looked innocent enough, but after a minute I went back inside and put on my tack-studded mantelet. After a moment's further consideration, I added the policeman's whistle and the sable muff with the revolver inside. Finally, with these defensive measures complete, I set off for Clerkenwell.

Almost immediately, a cabman stopped to offer his services. I waved him away without hesitation. When one has survived one murderous attack and hopes to avoid another, one does not take the first cab nor the second that presents itself. Indeed, since it was a pleasant day of mild temperature, hazy sunshine, and no wind, I thought it best not to take a cab at all, but to proceed on foot. The distance was not far, as Felicity had said, and I arrived at Miss Pring's lodging house in good time and with my smart apparel not in the least disarrayed.

The address Felicity had given me proved to be a large square house of liver-colored brick, one of a whole row of similar houses that had seen better days, but were still clinging tooth and nail to respectability. A maidservant who answered to the same description admitted me and showed me to a sitting room on the first floor.[4]

The room was clearly a private one, rather than a common parlour shared by other boarders. Looking around, I could see other signs of modest affluence: framed photographs; an engraving of the Queen; two prim chairs and a small sofa upholstered in slippery black horsehair; and a coffin-like bookcase filled with rows of weighty tomes. Despite these amenities, however, it was a chill

---

4 It would have been called the second floor in America. Here, as in so much else, the English system differs just enough to lay pitfalls for the unwary.—*Ed.*

and inhospitable little chamber. Not one thing in it was beautiful, or even attractive. There was an unrelenting quality to the furnishings—particularly noticeable in the chair I was sitting on—that I fancied might be expressive of the personality of the woman who owned them.

A moment later, Miss Pring entered the room, and I was able to ascertain it for myself.

For a woman she was tall and very thin. It was her thinness that chiefly struck me. There did not appear to be an ounce of superfluous flesh on her anywhere—or, indeed, much else that was superfluous about her appearance. Certainly she had nothing so superfluous as a smile for an unknown caller. She merely stood in the doorway of her sitting room, looking suspiciously from me to my visiting card.

"Miss Letitia Blackwood?" she said.

I inclined my head graciously. I find it convenient to use the name Letitia Blackwell on occasions when my professional name might appear out of place. Suffice to say it is no more my real name than the other, but "Letitia Blackwood" has a respectable ring to it, and I hoped the association with *Blackwood's Magazine* might support my literary pretensions.

Apparently both my name and my appearance passed muster, for Miss Pring's expression of suspicion abated slightly. "I don't believe I know you, Miss Blackwood?" she said, in a questioning voice. Though a trifle harsh in tone, it was unmistakably well-bred in its accents—almost painfully so.

"No, and I must beg your pardon for intruding in this manner, and without a proper introduction," I said, taking care to make my own voice as painfully genteel as hers. "My friend Sophronia Langley would, no doubt, have written me a letter of introduction, but I did not like to trouble her at such a time. As you may know, she has had a great sorrow lately . . .?"

"Ah, yes," said Miss Pring. I noted with interest that a spasm disfigured her face at the mere mention of the Langleys. It was not a well-favoured face even in repose, Dear Reader. We cannot help how our faces are made, but we can help how we use them, and Miss Pring's face had clearly been used to look sourly upon the world for at least the past sixty years.

"You may not have heard of me," I went on, in the modest accents of one who takes it for granted that hers is a household name. "I have some little reputation in educational circles. I am at present engaged in writing a work on the education of young women, and I was given your name as a possible source."

"My name?" said Miss Pring, looking surprised, but not—I was relieved to see—displeased.

"Yes, your name, ma'am. You have been an educator yourself, and if you have a few minutes to talk to me, I would be infinitely grateful. But perhaps now is not a convenient time?" I glanced around me with a pretence of concern.

This was the critical moment, Dear Reader. She might reject me and my advances, and if she did, there would be nothing to do but tamely go back home again. I was counting, however, on the fact that not only had she been a governess, she was a governess still in the eyes of the world. No elevation of rank had taken place to make her, like her fictional sister Jane Eyre, mistress of Thornfield Hall, or even the wife of some quite undistinguished man.

This is an important point, Dear Reader. You, like me, may have enjoyed the novels of Miss Charlotte and Anne Brontë with their governess heroines, but at the same time, you may also have been struck, like me, not so much by the romantic fate those heroines ultimately achieved, as by the misery of their daily lives so powerfully depicted by those gifted pens. In fact, neither Brontë sister achieved anything like real romance in her own life, but of loneliness and social ostracism they undoubtedly had their share. And the peculiar position of a governess in a wealthy household makes this very understandable.

Governesses are not considered members of the working class, but are rather what society is pleased to call ladies. They are paid a salary like servants; they are at the beck and call of their employers in the same way servants are; they may indeed receive substantially less pay for longer hours and harder work than servants in the same household. Yet all the while they cling to their superior social status, as somehow ennobling them beyond their fellow workers, while still being looked down upon by the people they serve. It is this tendency that has inspired Susan and Felicity with such a poor opinion of the race of governesses. Based on what I had heard of Miss Pring, I suspected she had it in spades.

And I proved to be perfectly right.

Even now, in her retirement, the poor woman was a prisoner of her own gentility. As soon as she was convinced of my status as a genuine Upper Class Lady worthy of her regard, I was taken to her bosom (such as it was). What was more, it took remarkably little to convince her. Normally, such a woman would never accept me solely on my own word—at least not without a lengthy cross-examination concerning my birth, family, and connections. But she was so desperate for company at this point that she skimmed right over these formalities. Sooner than I would have believed possible, I was seated beside her on her little sofa, and she was talking to me quite freely.

I soon understood why she so welcomed my company. She could not consort with the other women in her lodging house: "The woman who rooms next to me is really a most vulgar creature—very kind and well-meaning, I daresay, but I am continually having to depress her pretensions. She invited me to attend chapel with her last

Sunday—the very idea! Of course my family has always been High Church. And she drops her aitches, too."

Her landlady was similarly ineligible for friendship: "A very worthy woman, but you know her family was in *Trade*, and of course keeping a lodging house is not what one could call *genteel*. I take care to be perfectly polite in all my dealings with her, but nothing more. Such people are so very prone to presume upon any display of friendliness."

Indeed, it appeared I was the first person in years to be permitted to sit on Miss Pring's hard-sprung sofa and drink weak tea with her. I tried very hard to be grateful, Dear Reader. She was, after all, ready enough to give me the information I sought. It was simply a matter of directing the flow.

"The Langleys, yes—I was with them for years," said Miss Pring, when I ventured again to introduce their name into the conversation. "It was my last place, and a very good one. Only the one daughter, and everything done in the first style."

As she seemed about to enlarge on this last statement, I hastened to divert her. "How did you learn the Langleys needed a governess in the first place?" I asked.

It appeared that Miss Pring had been personally recommended to the Langleys by the family of a former pupil. "I was between positions at that point," she explained primly, "so I was willing to consider the offer Mr. Langley made to me."

I thought this was a grand way of saying she had been out of a job and willing to take whatever offered, but of course it is Human Nature to dress up Truth in this fashion. "I suppose you had an interview with Mrs. Langley also, before taking the position?" I asked.

"No, I only spoke to Mr. Langley," she said. "His wife was content to accept his judgment in the matter."

"Is that usual?" I asked.

She frowned a little, as though this were a point that had not previously occurred to her. "No, I would not say it was usual," she said. "Indeed, I am more accustomed to speaking to the maternal parent—or to both parents. But of course it is quite commendable for a father to take an interest in his daughter's education."

I could not bring myself to agree, Dear Reader. Innocently as she had meant her words, they were monstrous in light of my own knowledge. "I understand there was an Indian nursemaid who came before you," I said instead.

Her lips pursed at once into the expression that had probably inspired the Sterns to call her "Miss Prunes and Prisms." "Indeed, yes," she said. "There had been, in my opinion, a good deal of mismanagement in Miss Langley's early upbringing. I do not scruple to say this, for her father admitted it quite openly. The Coloured Races, you know, lack discipline. I could have told him that if he had consulted me, but I understand such arrangements are unfortunately common in India."

"And yet I had heard that Miss Langley was very attached to her ayah," I said—a trifle provocatively, I will admit.

Miss Pring made a noise that would have been a snort in a person less genteel. "Of course she was attached to her! She had been left to run wild and do exactly as she pleased. The ayah was lax—very lax. There had been no system, no order at all in Miss Langley's education up till the time I took over."

"Was she behind other children of her age?" I asked.

Miss Pring hesitated a little before answering. "No, I would not say that," she said at last, rather grudgingly. "She could read very well, and write well enough, and there had been some attempt to teach her simple arithmetic. But there had been no system in her education, as I said before. In her reading, for example, she was allowed to choose whatever she liked. Of course she preferred fairy stories, as is natural in a child of that age."

"Very natural," I agreed. "I take it you did not approve?"

"Certainly not," said Miss Pring, pursing her lips again. "I do not allow my pupils to waste their time on such trash. I made sure she had only good, improving books, and that her reading was restricted to regular hours."

Being myself an omnivorous and intemperate reader, I thought this the most appalling cruelty, but refrained from saying so. "If she had been left to run wild, as you say, then I suppose she chafed a bit at such discipline," I suggested.

"Yes, and that was to be expected. Fortunately, Mr. Langley had foreseen that it would be an issue."

"He did, did he?" I said, trying to keep the irony out of my voice.

"Yes, and that made my task much easier. You will understand how impossible it is to maintain discipline in the schoolroom, when one's authority is undermined by the parents of one's pupils."

"Yes, I can understand that."

"For myself, I have never allowed that sort of interference," said Miss Pring, with a look of proud consciousness. "I told Mr. Langley so quite frankly at our initial meeting. I told him that if we wished to undo the damage that had been done by years of over-indulgence, it would be necessary for both governess and parents to present a united front."

"Very sensible," I agreed. "And what specific measures did this entail?"

You will guess, Dear Reader, that I was hoping to get soon to the question of who had decreed that Elizabeth Langley should sleep alone in the dark. At the same time, I was trying not to do what in legal circles is called, I believe, leading the witness. If Miss Pring said anything that might be evidence, it would be more convincing if it came without any prompting from me.

It developed that there were a great many measures that Miss Pring had felt necessary to Miss Langley's moral and educational rehabilitation. If I had really been writing a book about educating young women, she would have given me material enough for a whole chapter. But just when I was thinking I would have to intervene to get her back on track, she electrified me by saying, "Then, too, I was obliged to give Miss Langley guidance in the matter of her friendships. She had developed intimacies with some of the local children whom Mr. Langley felt were quite unsuitable companions. He told me in confidence that he did not want them encouraged, and I quite agreed."

"Would these local children have been James and Cora Stern, by any chance?" I inquired.

Miss Pring admitted that they would be. "I may say that when I came to know them, I fully shared Mr. Langley's opinion. Most disrespectful children," she said, with her best Prunes-and-Prisms expression.

"So Mr. Langley did not wish his daughter to have friends?"

"No, he only wanted to keep her from having unsuitable ones."

"Did he then supply others, to take the place of the Sterns?" I asked.

Miss Pring seemed staggered by this question. "Really, I hardly know, Miss Blackwood," she said after a pause. "I cannot at the moment think of any, but I am sure he must have done. It stands to reason."

"He seems to have taken a great deal of interest in his daughter's affairs altogether," I said, watching her closely.

She agreed that this was the case, quite complacently. I longed to shake her out of her complacency. "I notice you do not mention Mrs. Langley taking the same kind of interest. Did she concur in all these measures you speak of?"

Miss Pring hesitated again before speaking. "Not entirely, no," she said. "She was a well-meaning woman, but like so many women, her maternal affection sometimes led her into ill-judged indulgences."

"What indulgences were these?"

"In the matter of the ayah, for one. If it had not been for Mr. Langley's firmness, I very much fear she would have allowed the ayah to stay on."

"And from your standpoint that would have been a mistake?"

"To be sure," said Miss Pring, looking surprised that there could be any question about it. "Indeed, it would have been better if Miss Langley had been under the care of a capable English nurse from the beginning. I was astonished to learn what had been allowed previous to my arrival. If you can believe it, the ayah actually slept in the night nursery with her young mistress!"

"I had heard something of that," I said carefully. "I presume you did not do the same?"

"Certainly not. I would regard any such arrangement as highly unsuitable. And in any case, the nursery floor was undergoing renovations at the time of my arrival."

"Ah," I said. "No more night nursery?"

"No, Miss Langley was getting to the age where it was more proper for her to have her own bedchamber."

"That was *your* judgment?" I said.

Miss Pring agreed that it was, in the same complacent tone. I could have slapped her. I was quite sure Charles Langley had had everything to do with the renovations to the nursery floor and his daughter's consequent change of rooms, but obviously he had had an accomplice made to order in Miss Pring. "After so many years of sharing a room with her ayah, it must have been hard for Miss Langley to adapt to a different arrangement," I suggested.

"Oh, yes," Miss Pring agreed quite readily. "But we had antici-
pated as much in the beginning, and so we stood firm."

"When you say 'we,' you mean . . .?"

"Mr. Langley and I," she said.

I felt we were getting somewhere at last. "And Mrs. Langley, too,
I presume?" I said softly.

The Prunes-and-Prisms look had appeared again on Miss Pring's
face. "I am afraid not. She would, I think, have given way to her
daughter's entreaties."

"Entreaties?" I said, raising my eyebrows. "Was her daughter so
very unhappy, then?"

Instead of answering this directly, Miss Pring stated that she did
not believe in indulging children's whims. "She was afraid of the
dark, as many children are, but of course that is merely a fancy. The
best way to overcome such fears is to face them directly."

I could hardly bear to ask the question. "And what exactly did
that entail in the case of Miss Langley?"

The answer was exactly what I had expected, Dear Reader. It had
entailed shutting her up in the dark and ignoring all her subsequent
cries for release—whatever might have prompted them. Moreover,
it developed that there had been claims of indefinite pain and illness
in the days that followed. "Of course children often plead illness to
get out of schoolwork. I do not condone that sort of malingering,
and so I told her."

"Did you never think she might really have been hurt in some
way?" I said, struggling to keep the anger out of my voice. "You
didn't think of calling in a doctor to see her?"

No, Miss Pring had not felt it necessary, and Mr. Langley had
quite agreed with her. "Miss Langley soon adjusted to the new regi-
men, and then we heard no more about her feeling unwell."

"Well," I said, "you certainly played an important rôle in her . . . development."

Miss Pring took this at face value and nodded solemnly. "Her parents were very pleased—most gratifyingly so. Mr. Langley insisted on making me a pension at the time I left their service. And a most generous pension, indeed! It enabled me to retire from teaching and to live most comfortably."

"Yes, so I see," I said. I could not resist adding, "It is a sad thing that Miss Langley did not long survive your retirement."

Once more a spasm crossed Miss Pring's face. "Yes," she said. "Most unfortunate."

Her face and voice both implied that it was the height of ill-breeding for her ex-pupil to have gotten herself killed in such a scandalous way. "We were all so shocked to learn of her death," I went on artlessly. "It must have been an even greater shock to you, who knew her so well."

"Yes," said Miss Pring. "A very great shock."

Her attitude was not encouraging, but I persevered. "Have you any opinion as to what could have happened to her?" I asked. "I understand the police are still investigating the matter."

"I cannot in the least imagine."

There was a finality in her voice that warned me I had better change the subject. I did so, unhappily reflecting that the scanty harvest of facts I had reaped so far was going to be all I got out of the afternoon.

Miss Pring soon regained her earlier good humour in telling me about her other teaching positions. I naturally had no interest in these, but feigned it successfully enough that Miss Pring was loath to let me go. She even suggested that I might stay to dinner if I had no other plans.

"My landlady keeps a very fair table, and as long as I let her know a little in advance, she is willing to provide enough for a guest."

"Thank you, but I must be going," I said, rising from the sofa in such haste that I came near to forgetting some of my belongings. Miss Pring helpfully pointed this out to me.

"You are forgetting your muff, Miss Blackwood. Good gracious, how heavy it is!"

I told her I kept my purse in it, Dear Reader. Let her imagine I was loaded down with golden sovereigns. It would, I thought, be the very least of her delusions.

CHAPTER 14

I could hardly wait to get home and tell Susan about my afternoon with Miss Pring. I did not know whether that would make me feel any better about it, but I thought it would be a relief to talk to someone who could at least see beyond the end of her own nose.

"Not a scrap of evidence," I said glumly, at the conclusion of my report. "And yet it's all highly suggestive."

"I should think so," agreed Susan. "A regular plot woven around the poor girl, seemingly."

"Yes, it's clear how it was done. The governess was simply a dupe. But she doesn't see it that way, and I don't believe anyone could make her see it now, after all this time. Another case of True Belief," I said, with a shake of my head. "The worst of it is that I can't help feeling a little sorry for her, too."

"I wouldn't waste any sympathy on *her*," said Susan. "All my sympathy's with poor Miss Langley."

I could understand Susan's viewpoint, Dear Reader. Indeed, to a certain extent I shared it. I myself had found Miss Pring an unsympathetic character, yet there was something pathetic about her all the same. Narrow-minded she might be; a bigot she certainly was; and to crown all she had been an accomplice (however unwittingly) in a terrible crime. Yet easy as I found it to condemn her, I also could not help thinking uneasily that there, but for the grace of God, might have gone Seraphina Fox.

For much as I disliked admitting it, there was a certain resemblance between the two of us. Although she was my elder by more than a decade, we had both left our youth behind without marrying. That meant we were considered by society as mere Old Maids—when society was kind enough to consider us at all.

Like Miss Pring, I had been well-educated, born to a moderate degree of privilege, yet forced to earn my own living. Only those who have found themselves in that same situation can appreciate how circumstances may work to shape our characters and our ends. If I had been raised by her people instead of mine, and made to earn my living the same way, might I not also have shared her prejudices and her follies? It is not often that I wax philosophical on subjects like these, Dear Reader, but at the moment, I could find it in my heart to pity Miss Pring as well as her unfortunate protégée.

"Everything she did, she did with the best intentions, however misguided," I told Susan. "She would be so aghast if she knew what she had been a party to. I couldn't bring myself to do more than hint at it, and even then it went right over her head."

I was still feeling unhappy about the situation at the breakfast table the next morning. Susan, in her sensible way, said I ought not to take it personally. "You're doing all you can. Felicity's doing all she can. And the poor Inspector, too, of course."

"Why feel sorry for him?" I retorted, stabbing at a piece of ham. "Here I am doing half his work for him. He never even thought of talking to Miss Pring."

"Well, but you didn't learn anything much from her, did you?"

"No, nothing of any value, I am afraid."

"Do you think he would have gotten anything more out of her?"

"Probably not as much," I admitted. I could not help smiling as I envisioned such an interview. "I am sure she thinks policemen are the Lowest of the Low. I doubt she would have told him anything at all."

"Well, then. Why fault him for neglecting his duty?"

"Because he doesn't seem to be accomplishing anything!" I said in exasperation. "He shows up here day after day, and yet he never has much to report in the way of progress."

Susan fixed me with a stern eye. "You might at least be kinder to the poor man," she said. "I do believe he's doing all he can. It about kills him that he can't find any evidence to tie Charles Langley to either murdering his daughter or attacking you."

"I daresay," I said shortly. I did have a certain sympathy for the Inspector, Dear Reader: more indeed than I allowed to show. But it does not do to encourage the police.

"I am grateful at least that he has largely succeeded in keeping the matter out of the newspapers," I went on, in an effort to be fair-minded. In one or two of the papers there had been a reference to an unnamed Spiritualist who had provided a clue in connection with the Elizabeth Langley affair, but nothing like the sensation the matter would have caused if the full facts were known. "But I daresay his reticence was motivated more on Charles Langley's account than on mine!"

Susan thought this unfair, and we were arguing the matter over when the doorbell rang. She went to answer it, while I retired to my bedroom. It was still early enough that I was wearing a simple wrapper rather than my full Spiritualistic regalia, and I don't like even casual callers to see me that way. Appearances are very important in my profession.

Susan came up while I was putting the finishing touches on my toilette. "It's a young woman," she said. "Her name's Jenny Taylor. Here's a note she said I should give to you."

I looked at the note, recognized Felicity's familiar handwriting, and felt my heart leap within my breast. Hastily breaking the seal, I opened it and read:

Seraphina, I send this child to you that she may tell her story in <u>*Person.*</u> *I don't know if 'twill help your* <u>*Cause*</u> *as she seems set against the idea of talking to the* <u>*Police.*</u> *But she was willing enough to tell me the* <u>*whole business,*</u> *and I think she'll tell it you, too. As it proved a* <u>*simple*</u> <u>*matter*</u> *to find her, I'll spare you my* <u>*usual fee,*</u> *but you might give her a pound or two if you're* <u>*so minded*</u>*. Yrs, F.*

To say the contents of this note astonished me would be an understatement. It was not that Felicity had succeeded in her task: for an agent of her abilities, failure would be more surprising. But that she was waiving her fee was something new. So was the abundance of underlined words in her message, which seemed to indicate that she was strongly moved. Giving a last adjustment to my veil-draped head, I left my bedroom and hurried down to the Sitting Room.

The young woman who was Jenny Taylor was sitting on the extreme edge of one of my Sitting Room chairs. She was tall, large-boned, and muscular, dressed in a shabby blue serge dress made up very plain. Her drab felt hat had no trimming at all, not even a simple ribbon. Her eyes and hair were dark, and she had one of those fair complexions deeply flushed with red that reminds one of raw beef. Beautiful she was not, but I am trained to look beyond the superficial, and I thought she looked both alert and intelligent.

She sprang to her feet as I entered the room. Her ungloved hands writhed and twisted together in her skirt front, betraying some nervousness, but her eyes were steady as she regarded me; and I could tell I was being evaluated in my turn.

"Good morning," I said. "I had your note—that is, the note you brought me." I showed her the note Felicity had written, then indicated the chair she had been sitting in. "Please be seated. Your name is Jenny Taylor?"

"That's right, ma'am," she said. Rather awkwardly she sat down, then scooted forward until she was once again on the extreme edge of the chair. I sat down opposite her on the sofa.

"And you work for the Langleys?"

Her face darkened. "I did, ma'am," she said. "I was nursery maid there at one time. But that was years ago. I've changed my place since then."

I judged her age to be about twenty-two or –three, Dear Reader. That was not old enough to have changed her place many times in the ordinary course of things. "Was the Langleys' your first place?" I asked.

"Yes, ma'am," she said tersely.

"And when did you leave there?"

"It's been a bit more'n three years, ma'am. But I didn't leave of my own accord. I was let go—and unfairly let go, to my way of thinking."

I studied her with interest. There had been a flash of anger in her eyes as she spoke of being let go. Clearly there was bad blood between her and her former employer. This boded well for my purposes. "I wish you would tell me all about it," I said.

But it wasn't going to be that easy. "About what, ma'am?" she asked, with the stolid stupidity servants are so well able to assume.

I hesitated. Clearly Felicity had drawn some story out of her that was germane to my purposes. "About how you came to get hired on with the Langleys, to start with," I said. "And what your duties were there."

She obediently told me how she had applied for the post and been accepted on a six-months' trial. "How old were you at the time?" I asked.

"I was ten, ma'am," she said, and again I saw a flash of anger in her eyes. "As I say, it was my first post, and a pretty hard one at that, but I was used to working hard at home. It wasn't any worse'n that was. The food was good, too—better'n what we had at home, and they didn't stint you. I kept the nursery swept and clean and waited on Miss Elizabeth and her ayah." She looked at me a bit anxiously, obviously uncertain whether "ayah" was a word I understood. "That's like a nurse, in India. The family had lived in India, and Miss Elizabeth had been born there, and the ayah had come back to England with them."

I nodded to show my understanding. "You have heard about this sad business of Miss Elizabeth's being found dead?"

"Yes, ma'am," she said, and her face twisted for a moment in what looked like genuine grief. "I was real sorry to hear about that."

"Well, as you may have heard, I am looking into her death. The police have been investigating it, of course, but I have reason to think they are on the wrong track."

I studied her to see her reaction to this, and she looked back at me with that same expression of bovine stupidity. "I myself am nothing to do with the police," I went on, laying a stress on the words. "I have personal reasons for wanting to punish whoever hurt Miss Elizabeth. Anything you tell me, I will promise to keep confidential." I was well aware this might be a promise I couldn't keep, Dear Reader, but one must trust to fortune for something. I wasn't going to be baulked of getting the information I needed, even if it might be a puzzle how to use it later.

In any case, Miss Taylor didn't seem impressed by my words. She just sat looking at me, waiting for me to go on. Since she had shown a flash of emotion at the mention of Elizabeth Langley, I thought this might be the place to apply the lever. "In order to learn who killed Miss Elizabeth, I have been trying to find out more about her past. I feel quite sure this whole matter has its roots in the past."

She merely nodded, her expression guarded. "You must have known her pretty well if you were her nursery maid," I went on. "Was she a difficult child to deal with?"

"Difficult?" repeated Miss Taylor. Her face twitched into a brief smile. "Well, she had a mind of her own, but no, I wouldn't call her difficult. No, she was a real sweet little thing, albeit she'd been badly spoiled."

"I understand her parents gave her everything she wanted— when she was little," I said. "But it was different when she got older, wasn't it?"

At first I thought Miss Taylor wasn't going to answer. At last, slowly, she said, "You mean about them sending away her ayah?"

"Yes," I said. "That was her father's doing, as I understand it. And I wondered about that. Everyone has told me how upset she was when her ayah was sent away."

Miss Taylor merely looked at me, poker-faced. I threw another card on the table. "Mrs. Langley said the ayah was bullied by the other servants, and that she suffered from the cold here in England. Do you think that's why she went back to India?"

"No," said Miss Taylor. Although it was a flat no, it was also an authoritative one, and my heart quickened.

"Do you think Miss Elizabeth's father sent her away deliberately?"

"Yes." Once again, there was authority in the monosyllable.

"And do you think he had his own private reason for wanting the ayah gone?"

"Yes," said Miss Taylor. "And I knew what it was, when I saw the blood on the sheets."

I looked at her. Her ruddy face had flushed to an even deeper hue, and there was a fierce light in her eyes. "I knew what he was doing then. Because he'd done it to me, too, d'you see."

I stared at her, open-mouthed. She went on, the words spilling out as if some dam had been breached with her first admission. "He did it with all the girls—the servant girls, I mean. And then he did it with his own daughter. His own daughter, ma'am! I wouldn't have believed it, but I saw the blood, and I knew. That's why he sent the ayah away. The governess that came after—she wouldn't have known what was going on, even if it happened under her nose. But I knew. Well, she was the right age—around ten or so—and he liked them young, the filthy swine." She paused, looking at me defiantly.

I could not help feeling sickened, Dear Reader. Of course one is aware that such things go on. If one traverses the streets of London at night, one will see quite a number of what are called Women of Easy Virtue, many of whom are not women at all, but mere girls. There is a market for such wares, and no lack of unscrupulous folk to supply it. Doubtless some of the girls even embrace the life of their own accord, out of simple necessity. Not every woman is lucky enough to have a trade, even such a disreputable one as Spiritualism.

When I spoke, I was careful to keep my voice matter-of-fact. "I had suspected Mr. Langley was abusing his daughter in that way. But I did not realize he had other victims."

"Oh, yes, ma'am," said Miss Taylor. "I wasn't the first nor the last. But as I say, I couldn't believe he'd do it to his own daughter."

It was easy to see the distinction was important to her, though it seemed almost immaterial to me. "Yes," I said. "And then he killed her. For I am sure that's what happened. She was about to be married, and I think he was afraid that she would tell her future husband that he was molesting her."

To my surprise, Miss Taylor shook her head. "Oh, he wouldn't have been doing it then," she said. "He'd have stopped once she started her monthly courses. So he wouldn't get her pregnant," she explained. "That's how he did with the rest of us."

It made sense, Dear Reader, in a sickening kind of way. "Then he must have been afraid she would tell her future husband that he had molested her in the past—that she wasn't a virgin anymore."

Miss Taylor nodded, her expression grim. "That's it," she said. "That's what he would have been afraid of."

"You must feel lucky that he didn't treat you the same way," I suggested, curious to know her thoughts on the matter.

"Lucky!" she repeated. It sounded like an explosion. "He didn't need to kill *me* to keep my mouth shut. He knew well enough I'd never dare breathe a word of it. Not to the police at any rate, or to anyone who'd be able to stop him." She looked at me, and there was a strange mixture of hope and skepticism in her eyes. "Do you think you're going to be able to stop him, ma'am?"

"I'm certainly going to try," I said, as firmly as I could.

"If you could, ma'am! Oh, if you could!" Grief and rage mingled in her voice, and again the words poured out in a torrent. "I'm not a smart girl, or a pretty girl. I haven't had any advantages at all. I can write my own name, and read my orders in the housekeeper's book, and that's about all, so far as learning goes. I work from before sunrise to past sunset, with a half day off alternate weeks, and it's hard physical work—I'm naught but a housemaid, and never going to rise any higher. If I'm *lucky*," she said, and again she laid a scathing stress on the word, "if I'm lucky and my health don't break down, I'll keep doing it till I die. My one chance to get out of it—my *only* chance to get out of it—is if I can find a good man to marry me. And no good man would have me, if he knew I wasn't a maid. It's as simple as that."

"That's why you can't go to the police," I said, seeing it with a terrible clarity.

"That's right, ma'am. 'Twould be my word against his in any case, and who do you think they'd believe? And even if they did believe me, I'd be ruined—ruined just the same." She looked at me with smouldering eyes. "I think sometimes it'd be easier just to make an end of myself. But if I do, I'll make an end of him first. I dream about it sometimes. My virtue was about all I had, and he took it from me. I'd like to see him burn in Hell."

I was feeling the same way at this point. "We must see if we can't bring his crimes home to him," I said. "If you would be willing to tell this to the police—"

"Not the police," she said instantly. "I won't talk to the police. I'd sooner throw myself in the river. You promised, ma'am—you promised it wouldn't go no further. I wouldn't have talked to you else."

"Very well," I said, since she seemed adamant on this point. "I did promise, and I certainly don't want you to throw yourself in the river. I want you to be alive and well and able to drink a toast to celebrate when we bring Mr. Charles Langley to justice."

She smiled at the thought, but her face soon shadowed again. "Forgive me for my plain speaking, ma'am, but I misdoubt you'll do it," she said. "He's a rich man, and everyone knows there's one law for the rich and another for the poor."

I told her bracingly that it wasn't quite as bad as that, although certainly the law was less equably enforced than might be desired. "The police inspector in charge of the case is trying hard to see that justice is done. Have you talked to him at all?"

"No, ma'am," she said, shaking her head vigourously. "I never talked to him. And I wouldn't have told him anything if I had."

Her last statement was no more than I expected, but the first one surprised me. "He didn't talk to you at all?" I repeated. "But of course—you wouldn't have been working for the Langleys by the time the police got around to questioning the servants."

"No, ma'am," she said again. "I was let go, as I told you. On a trumped-up excuse." Her voice was bitter as she added, "It was him that was behind it—I know it was. He'd used me, and then he got rid of me."

I wrinkled my forehead at this. "But you worked there for how long? Eight years?"

"Aye, Eight years, almost to the day."

"And you say he left you alone after you started your monthly courses?"

She nodded.

"And when was that?"

"I was fourteen, ma'am."

"So he kept you around for four years after that."

I looked at her, but she merely looked back at me, not seeming to grasp the significance of the point. I tried again. "Did he get rid of the other girls after he used them?"

"No, ma'am. He was safe enough keeping them around, knowing they couldn't open their mouths without losing their places and their reputations."

"But then why did he get rid of you?" I asked. "Wouldn't the same objection apply to you?" I was beginning to wonder if Miss Taylor might have been misled on this particular point—or if possibly she was trying to mislead *me*. Perhaps in her rage against her former employer, she was unjustly blaming him for this lesser crime. "If what you say is true," I went on, watching her carefully, "why didn't he get rid of you immediately? Why did he wait four years?"

She looked at me somberly. "I think it was because he'd made up his mind to kill Miss Elizabeth. And he thought I might put two and two together, being her maid and all. I was let go just a few days afore she disappeared. I didn't realize it at the time, because for a long time we didn't know what had happened to her. The story I heard said she'd run away with someone. But when I heard she'd been found dead, well, I started thinking about it, and I realized that's why I was fired off when I was."

It made perfect sense to me, Dear Reader. Indeed, it had the inevitable feel of the truth. "In that case, we might be able to prove it," I said with some excitement. "There must be a record of your being fired. The other servants would know when it was, and what the reason was supposed to be, and if he was behind it."

She was already shaking her head. "It wouldn't be enough," she said. "Even if I was to go in front of a magistrate and say everything I've said to you, it wouldn't be enough. And I'm not about to do that."

I couldn't blame her, but it was inconvenient. "Very well," I said. "What you've told me helps immeasurably in any case."

She responded by saying she hoped it would help get Charles Langley hanged. "You must think I'm very wicked, saying such things," she added, looking at me defiantly. "I know it's not Christian. But what he did to me—and to the others—and then to his own daughter! It seems to me hanging's too good for him."

I did not think she was wicked at all, Dear Reader, but rather remarkably forbearing. The common people of England never revolted like the French, but anyone could see this girl was ripe for revolution. I had no trouble imagining her at the head of a mob howling for the blood of Charles Langley and his ilk. It would have made a striking picture, too. With the fire of anger burning in her eye, she was by no means as plain as she had first appeared. With her impressive height and build, she would have made a very fair model for an English version of *Liberty Leading the People*.

After a little more desultory conversation, she said she had to go, and I agreed that she must. "I appreciate your coming to me this way, in the little free time you have," I told her. "This is your half-day?"

"Yes, ma'am," she said. "I had to wait till today to come round and see you, like the other lady told me to. The one who wrote the note there." She nodded at Felicity's note.

"And you don't get another half day for two more weeks?"

"No, ma'am." She shook her head. "And I must be getting back soon. It's as much as my place is worth to stay out an hour over my time."

"Then you must allow me to make it up to you," I said.

Reader, I gave her twenty pounds. She demurred at first, saying all she wanted was to see Charles Langley brought to justice and that she'd rather the money be used for that. When I tell you that twenty pounds was twice her annual salary as a housemaid, you will understand, perhaps, the full depth of her anger.

CHAPTER 15

After Jenny Taylor had left, I collapsed into a chair. Susan, who had shown her to the door, came into the Sitting Room and sat down opposite me. Her face was like a thundercloud. "Poor girl," she said.

"My God, yes," I said. "Did you get all that written down?"

"Most of it. She talked a bit fast for me in places, but I got the meaning of it all right."

"Now what am I to do with it?" I demanded. "You heard her. She won't talk to the police. I'm quite sure her death would be on my head if I tried to make her."

"Yes," agreed Susan, but got no further. The doorbell rang again. We looked at each other.

"If it's the Inspector, tell him I'm out. Even if he knows I'm in—thanks to his odious police watch—tell him I'm out. I must have time to think about this."

I fled to my bedroom, but when Susan arrived a minute later, she informed me it wasn't the Inspector after all. "It's Mrs. Langley. Will you see her?"

"It needed only this," I said bitterly.

Susan waited while I paced the floor, irresolute. Finally, I decided I might as well talk to Mrs. Langley. "We're at a standstill now. Perhaps she will give me a clue how to proceed."

When I came down to the Sitting Room again, I found Mrs. Langley in the same chair Jenny Taylor had vacated so short a time before. Like mistress, like maid. I am not a soft-hearted woman, but at that moment I wasn't sure whom I felt most sorry for.

"Madame Fox," she said, rising at my entrance and coming forward to take my hand between her own, as was her custom. "Thank you for seeing me. Perhaps you can guess why I am here."

I could guess very easily, of course. After I had refused her last plea for another séance, she had expressed the hope that I might change my mind if the police failed to make any progress in finding her daughter's killer. Certainly they had made no progress, and now here she was again, her haunted eyes full of hope as she looked at me.

I murmured something about being pleased to see her at any time. She brushed this aside as the triviality it was. "The police inspector has told me that the investigation stands much as it did before," she said. "Apparently they have still found no evidence to show who is responsible for my daughter's death. That being the case, I hoped you might be willing to sit for me again. We had such a miraculous result last time. I cannot forbear hoping that a second sitting might solve the whole mystery."

I looked at her in wonderment, but she appeared to be perfectly serious. "Would you call it miraculous?" I asked in a faint voice.

She nodded, looking surprised at the question. "Yes, of course! After being so long in suspense, to finally know the truth—or some part of the truth, at least. Yes, it was a miracle."

"But it was a very painful truth," I pointed out.

"Yes, I would not deny that. Very painful." She looked down at her black dress with its trimming of crape. "But it is better to know the truth, I think, even if it *is* painful, than to go forever in suspense."

I nodded, but couldn't help thinking that the truth thus far revealed to her wasn't a patch on what still remained hidden. She studied me, her expression perplexed. "I know it was a great strain on your . . . on your special powers last time. I understand your reluctance to undergo such a strain again. But if I could prevail upon you to make the effort, Madame Fox! Oh, you would have my eternal gratitude."

"Even if I failed to discover the truth?" I questioned.

"Even then, of course. But I feel certain you would not fail. From the beginning, it has been you who have held the key to this mystery. I felt it, the first time I laid eyes on you."

If she could have foreseen such a result from our first encounter, I felt she must have greater Spiritualistic powers than I did. But of course she did not know the full extent of the mystery, or how horribly its solution would rebound upon her. "I would be sorry, ma'am, to disappoint you," I said carefully. "But I don't think you have given this matter enough thought. Some truths are *better* hidden. What I mean is—painful as it has been for you thus far, I think a full explication of the matter might be worse."

She gazed at me, her expression of perplexity gradually changing to one of conviction. "You know something," she said.

"No, only guess it," I said, honestly enough.

"But can you not tell me? If you could understand the torment I feel!"

"I do understand it, ma'am. I am afraid telling you would only make it worse."

"No," she said with certainty. "Nothing could be worse than not knowing."

She seemed very sure, but then she didn't know how much worse it really was. In any case, I had no proof that would convince her, if for any reason she baulked at my solution. "I cannot justify divulging what is only a guess," I said, hedging.

She considered a moment, then nodded. "Very well. I must accept that, if you say it is so. But in that case, it seems to me another sitting might be the way to confirm this guess of yours. Would you not do it for me? For me, Elizabeth's mother?"

I could not resist, Dear Reader; I had to ask. "What does your husband think of the idea?"

She frowned. "He is not in favour," she admitted. "He is—was—not a believer in Spiritualism. After what happened the other night, of course he had to accept that there is something in it, but it goes hard with him. He had convinced himself that Elizabeth had merely run away. It was a great shock to him, to have it proved otherwise."

I didn't doubt that for a minute.

"But naturally he would take part if we had another sitting, Madame Fox. Indeed, he could hardly refuse to do so! For he is as eager to know the truth as I am."

The idea came to me then, in all its dubious glory. I looked at her, weighing the consequences in my mind. She had said I was the key to solving the mystery. Very possibly she was right, if I were willing to grasp the nettle. It was a particularly thorny nettle, however, and I wanted time to think about it. It meant risking not only my livelihood but my life, for I was under no illusions about Mr. Langley's being a dangerous and unscrupulous man.

"I cannot give you a decision now," I told her. "Let me consult the Spirits tonight and ask for guidance. I will let you know the answer tomorrow."

∞⟵ ⟶∞

After she was gone, I staggered down to the kitchen and sat down at the table, putting my head in my hands. Susan joined me there. After taking one look at me, she set about making a pot of tea. She did not speak until I had accepted a cup, drunk it off, and leaned back in my chair.

"You're thinking about doing another sitting for her?" she queried.

I nodded.

"Do you think the wheel'll spell out the truth, then? Like it did last time?"

I shook my head. "No," I said. "I don't think that will ever happen again."

She eyed me carefully. "Then what do you hope *will* happen?"

I told her. She was naturally aghast.

"You've gone mad! Even if it were to work—and that's a mighty big if—it'd mean the police would be on to you. They'd know you were a fraud."

"They suspect it anyway," I pointed out.

"Yes, but they don't *know*. You remember what the Inspector said. He said it was just a working assumption that you were a fraud, but that he didn't mean to give you trouble if you didn't step over the line. But if you do this, he'll have to take notice. I don't see how he could help himself."

"Probably not," I agreed. "I wish I could think of some other way to settle the matter, but I can't. This plan's uncertain enough as it is."

"But even if you make it work, you'd have to leave London!"

I winced. That was certainly the weak point in my scheme, Dear Reader. For I had come to love London. I loved my *bijou* little Temple, and my comfortable way of life, and the luxury of having a settled residence after so many years of peripatetic wandering. "Look on the bright side," I suggested. "I might not survive the experiment, and then the whole point will be moot."

Susan said disapprovingly that it wasn't a joking matter. I could understand her attitude, of course. It would mean the end of a comfortable way of life for her, too. "Don't worry, Susan," I said, patting her hand. "If I do survive and have to leave London, I'm not about to leave you behind. You are the very best assistant I have ever had. Although mine is the showier and more public rôle, I couldn't manage without your support behind the scenes."

Susan was so affected by this speech that she actually shed a few tears. I ended up shedding a few, too, and got eye-black all over my handkerchief. "You've never had a chance to travel like I have," I went on, between sniffs. "Well, this will be an opportunity for you to see a bit of the world. I was thinking perhaps the Continent. We'd have to stay away from France, of course, but I understand the Low Countries are very pleasant, and that one can live very cheaply there."

Susan, with a Londoner's sturdy insularity, said she didn't care tuppence about seeing the Low Countries. "I'd much rather stay right here," she declared. "I do wish you'd think this through, ma'am. I don't know what's got into you. Throughout this whole business, you've been acting totally contrary to what you've always told me is the sensible way to go on."

I couldn't deny it, Dear Reader. That circumstance had struck me, too. "I suppose it's thinking about that poor girl—Elizabeth Langley, I mean. And now that other poor girl today: Jenny Taylor. The man's a monster, and no one else seems able to stop him. Did I tell you that Felicity waived her fee, after hearing what happened to Jenny? Felicity! You know she's a businesswoman to her fingertips. Yet she was moved enough to contribute her mite. And Jenny herself, wanting to use that twenty pounds I gave her, when her shoes want resoling, and her dress is ready for the ragbag. I feel I must do *something*."

Susan admitted that she, too, would like very well to see Mr. Langley get his comeuppance. "But surely there's some other way to do it, that wouldn't involve risking your business?"

I put my head in my hands again. "I wish there were. But I keep thinking Mrs. Langley's right and I'm the key to the whole business."

Susan said I was merely dramatizing myself. "As usual," she added. I don't believe this is true, Dear Reader, but I include it for what it is worth. "I daresay if you'll only sit tight, the police'll get the case solved sooner or later."

I couldn't think so myself, Dear Reader. In any case, unless they solved it quickly, my business was going to suffer. In fact, it already *had* suffered. When I thought it over, I could see it was that, as much as anything, that made me feel I had to act.

You may laugh at me for saying so, but in my heart of hearts, I regard myself as an artist. My work is my art. Common fraudsters and confidence men may use some of the same tricks I do, yet I have always tried to make my sessions with the Spiritograph not only profitable to me but inspiring and uplifting to my clients. I want them to go away from the Temple of Spiritualism feeling moved even to tears, but happy with the conviction of a vague but beautiful future existence to comfort them. If I withhold their Loved Ones' trinkets, it is only to give them back again with their value enhanced. If I tell them lies, they are at least hopeful lies that soften the mystery of the death we all must face. You may say that I do it for the money, and I cannot gainsay it. But I get a satisfaction beyond the money from doing it *well*.

For ten years now I had worked at building and refining my trade, plying it to my own satisfaction as well as my clients'. And then Charles Langley had come into my little Elysium, and he had brought ugliness with him. And the ugliness had grown greater with each day and with each revelation of his character. If I did nothing to stop him, that ugliness would continue to live and thrive, and it would taint everything. I wouldn't be able to think of myself—my Temple—even of London itself—with the same satisfaction.

That being the case, it seemed worth it to throw everything I had into what might be my final performance.

By final performance, of course, I meant final performance in London. Yet given Charles Langley's murderous proclivities, I had to prepare myself also for the possibility that it might be my final performance on Earth. That was taking a dim view of it, however. I have some little experience in these matters, and I meant to take precautions. And the first step was to take Inspector Harper into my confidence.

CHAPTER 16

Although I was eager to see the Inspector, I had no wish for him to see me looking like a pink-nosed raccoon, which is what I resembled after crying. I hurried to touch up the shadows around my eyes and to re-powder my nose. I also took time to change into a new and elegant dress of black lace over smoke-grey satin. I was quite ready by late afternoon, his usual time of calling, but he did not come at the usual time. I waited and waited, postponing dinner until it was almost spoiled, and then, to Susan's disgust, eating hardly any of it. I knew that once I spoke to the Inspector, I would be committed to my plan of action, and I was too wrought up by the idea to have much appetite.

I had Susan light the lamps in the Sitting Room in readiness for his visit. I told her to be ready with the tea-tray when I rang. I also told her there would be no need for her to take notes during this interview. She had had a strenuous afternoon of note-taking already. But an hour went by, and then another, with no sign of Inspector Harper or even of P.C. Shaw.

When the doorbell rang around nine o'clock, I sprang up to answer it myself. Instead of Inspector Harper, however, it proved to be a gentleman swollen of jaw and redolent of cloves, who had mistaken my business for that of the dentist next door. Anyone compelled to seek a dentist at that hour is deserving of sympathy from his fellow men and women, Dear Reader, but I am afraid I dealt with him rather shortly.

"Try the next door down," I said, and shut the door in his swollen face.

I had almost given up hope of seeing the Inspector that evening when at last the door-bell rang again. I let Susan answer it this time, and a moment later heard Inspector Harper's familiar step in the corridor.

As you may imagine, having been obliged to wait hours to impart my momentous decision, I was nearly ready to explode with it. But as the Inspector seated himself in his usual chair in my Sitting Room, I could see that he, too, was wrought up as with some internal struggle. So I merely offered him a cup of tea.

"Well," he said hesitantly, "I'm off duty now, so—yes, that would be very welcome." He ran a hand through his hair. "Very welcome indeed. I didn't have a minute for lunch, and it's so late now that I doubt I'll get dinner either. My landlady doesn't welcome meals out of hours."

"Then she was ill-advised to accept a policeman as a lodger," I said, as I rang the bell. When Susan appeared, I told her to bring not only the tea-tray, but the roast chicken left over from dinner and any bread and cheese P.C. Shaw might have overlooked in the course of his nightly depredations. The Inspector made no objection, and when I mentioned that he looked as though he could use something stronger than tea, he admitted that a brandy and soda would not come amiss. I had Susan mix one for myself as well, purely to be sociable. After he had drunk about half of his, he glanced up with a strained expression.

"You will be wanting to hear what progress we have made on the case," he said. "I wish I had better news to report."

"No progress, then?" I said.

"Rather the reverse." He looked at me unhappily. "The Chief thinks we're on the wrong line altogether. He doesn't believe I'm justified in keeping my men tied up watching this place any longer. That means I won't be able to have Shaw stay nights here any longer, either. I know you've complained about our presence, but I tell you I don't like the idea of leaving you without any protection at all. I believe your theory, even if the Chief doesn't, and I don't trust Langley. I think you're right that he was the one who attacked you the other night. I hope you will believe me when I say how sorry I am."

"Of course," I said. I waited, but he showed no sign of saying anything more. He merely sat drinking his brandy and soda with a gloomy expression. "Is that all?" I asked.

"Isn't that enough?" he said with some surprise.

"I only wanted to make sure you were done telling me all you had to say," I explained. "Because I have something to say, too."

It was obvious he had been in too much of a funk to utilize his usual powers of observation. At these words he looked at me sharply, and his expression focused with sudden interest. "What is it? What's happened?"

"I had another caller today," I said. "Two callers, in fact, but I believe you will find the first one the more interesting."

Thanks to his late arrival, I had had plenty of time to transcribe Jenny Taylor's statement into longhand. I gave it to him complete, omitting only the mention of her name.

He read it, then dropped it in his lap. "Dear God," he said, looking equal parts stunned and sickened.

"The man is a monster," I said.

"I don't disagree. Well, this puts a different complexion on things."

"Do you think so?"

"Yes, indeed. If he's a habitual offender in this respect, there must be some evidence we can get. This girl—you don't give her name, I notice—"

"No," I said. "I am sure you could find it out easily enough, but she doesn't want to speak to the police, as she says in the transcript."

"Well, I appreciate her reservations, but she's got to speak to us. She's an important witness."

"She says she would rather throw herself in the river," I said, my voice sharpening. "And I promised that if she told me, I would make sure she didn't have to."

"That's all very well, but you weren't in a position to make such a promise," said the Inspector, his voice sharpening likewise.

"She won't talk to you in any case," I shot back. "She doesn't have any confidence that her story would be believed. And I fear she is only too right. Can you see twelve unimaginative English jurymen believing Charles Langley, the wealthy, successful man of affairs, could have committed such an act? She's a servant—a lower servant at that, with no education and far from perfect grammar. She was fired by Langley for neglect of her duties. That would discredit her testimony right there. The jury would believe she was making it all up to get back at him. Or they'd believe she was no better than she ought to be in the first place, and that he merely enjoyed one of those little trysts with the female staff that most Englishmen are perfectly willing to condone."

"Not most Englishmen," protested the Inspector. "No decent man would take advantage of a woman in that situation, even leaving ordinary morality out of the question. She would be a dependent under his roof, who wouldn't feel free to refuse him without fear of repercussions."

This struck me as highly idealistic, Dear Reader, but I thought none the worse of him for that. Upholders of the Law ought to be idealistic, if only to keep them from degenerating into bullies. "Most Englishmen of Charles Langley's class would condone it, then," I said, humouring him. "In any case, she would be publicly branded as a light woman, and then what would become of her? Do you know how difficult it is for a woman in her situation to find a decent position anyway? If you can call it decent, slaving seven days a week for a pittance. And with marriage her only hope of escape, and that hope gone as soon as she tells the world what Langley did to her."

The Inspector was looking more and more unhappy. "Yes, I read what she said. Poor girl, I wish I could say she wasn't right. But the penalty for that kind of transgression—even when it's a willing transgression on both sides—does tend to fall more heavily on the woman in the case."

"You mustn't bring her into this," I urged. "After all, you never would have known she existed, if I hadn't brought her to your attention."

"That is true," said the Inspector, looking unhappier yet. "I was remiss not to have thought of talking to Langley's former servants as well as his present ones. But she was let go before Elizabeth Langley disappeared, just as she says herself. I had no reason to think a discharged nursery maid, or in fact any of the Langleys' past servants, could shed light on her disappearance. Nonetheless, it was remiss of me not to think of it."

"My witness wouldn't have told you anything anyway."

"Perhaps not," he said. I looked at him, my brows raised, and he gave me a brief, strained smile. "Very well: I grant that you are right, Madame Fox. She wouldn't have told me anything. This is one of those cases where you have gotten a result we never could have. I am very much obliged to you, only I don't see how I am to use this information if I can't even talk to the witness, much less put her on the witness stand."

"I have been thinking about that," I said. "It doesn't seem as though there's any way for the police to use the information. But I wondered if perhaps I might be able to."

He looked at me sharply. "How? What do you mean?"

"Mrs. Langley also called here today. She is still wanting me to have another sitting, to determine who killed her daughter."

He thought about this, and I could see he had grasped the germ of the idea, but his expression was skeptical. "I don't see how that is likely to help. No matter what comes out of it, the jury isn't likely to be more impressed by the word of Spirits than by your discharged maidservant."

"No, I realize that," I said. "But tell me this, Inspector. What kind of evidence would it take to make a convincing case against Langley?"

"What kind of evidence?" he repeated. "Well, for this type of crime, an eyewitness who saw him having an altercation with his daughter—or saw him actually murdering her—or saw him with her dead body. Next best would be someone who saw him near the crypt, along with evidence he had been digging. Or someone who saw him when he tried to strangle you the other night."

"First-hand testimony of an eyewitness?"

"That would be best, of course. But I'd also take the word of a conspirator who helped him—or even someone who overheard him talking about killing her, or burying her, or attacking you. That'd only be hearsay, but I'd be glad to have it in this case, where there's precious little else to go on."

"What about a confession from the man himself?"

He went very still, like a cat that glimpses movement within a mouse-hole. I could see he understood me perfectly now. "Oh, no," he said. "I see what you're getting at, but I don't think so. In the first place, it wouldn't be safe. And in the second place, it's against police procedure. We can't let people talk without cautioning them that the evidence might be used against them."

"The police can't. But if I could? And you were listening while I did it?"

He shook his head, regarding me with bemusement. "It would be highly irregular," he said. "Besides, I can't believe anything would come of it. He's a cold-blooded man who has no compunction about debauching little girls, including his own daughter. We have compelling evidence he murdered her and then tried to murder you, and you think he is likely to confess? He'd be more likely to try to strangle you again!"

"Yes, I thought of that," I said, nodding. "And if he did, then you could arrest him for it."

"Now listen here," said the Inspector, with a flush of colour in his cheeks, "listen here! Even to get evidence against Langley, do you think I would agree to such a plan? Using you as 'a tethered goat to catch a tiger,' wasn't it?"

"It's different this time," I said. "This time I am volunteering."

"And it's a very noble gesture." He looked at me with so much admiration that I felt compelled to dispel it.

"Not at all," I said. "I am simply tired of this stalemate. The man is a menace, and no one else seems able to stop him. I thought I could at least try."

The Inspector pondered. "Very well," he said. "For argument's sake, let's say I let you try. You plan to hold another sitting as you did before?"

"Yes, but this time you would be there to see and hear what happens."

"Ah, but that wouldn't be enough," he said, shaking his head. "Not in the case of a confession, at least. Legally, we'd be open to all kinds of questions from defending counsel, what with my being on the force. For something like that, we would want a few solid citizens of good reputation—citizens with no connection to the police—who would also be there to witness the confession and testify the police didn't extort it."

"As to that, there would be no difficulty at all. Mr. Roland was at the last sitting, and I don't doubt he could be persuaded to attend again. And perhaps Mr. Stern would attend as well. He seems eager enough to see himself cleared."

The Inspector considered this judicially, then nodded. "Yes, that might pass, if Langley did confess. But I cannot believe he would. Or that you believe he would, either." He looked at me with skepticism. "You must have great confidence in your Spiritualistic powers."

Now it was my turn to flush. "It doesn't matter what you or I believe, Inspector Harper. What matters is what Charles Langley believes. You said it yourself, not so very long ago. He believes I conjured up the Spirit of his daughter last time, and he is so worried that I might do it again that he tried to kill me to prevent it."

"That does argue a pretty powerful belief," conceded the Inspector. "But it sounds as though what happened last time was—well, an anomaly. Wasn't it? The first time I talked to you, you as good as admitted it was. What happens if the Spirits don't cooperate this time around?"

Now we were on shaky ground. I very much disliked putting the whole thing baldly into words, but I forged ahead nonetheless. "That is a possibility, so I would have to be prepared for it. If no genuine Spirit materializes, then I would have to make him believe one had."

"To falsify it," he said, putting it into words yet balder.

"Yes," I said.

There was a little pause, and then he asked the question I had been dreading. "How would you do that?"

"Well," I said carefully, "you and I both know that there are such things as fraudulent Spiritualists. They falsify this kind of phenomena all the time. So there are ways to do it, and I am sure if I put my mind to it, I would be able to think of a way to make my wheel spell out answers even if there is no Spirit there to move it."

I hoped this would be enough for him, and happily it was. "And you could make the wheel spell out some accusation that Charles Langley might respond to?"

"I think I could."

"It still seems a long chance to me. To make a man like that lose his head and incriminate himself—"

"You weren't there last time. You have no idea how eerie it was. He was sobbing like a child afterwards."

Again the Inspector pondered. "But this time he would be prepared for it. He might not respond."

"I think I can prod him into doing something, even if it's merely attacking me. He wouldn't like having his guilt put into words in front of his wife and Mr. Roland and Mr. Stern."

"No, he wouldn't, would he?" The Inspector looked at me with an expression of awe. "But I can't believe you would be willing to take such a risk. And I'm not sure I ought to let you."

"You cannot stop me," I said. Seeing his face, however, I relented enough to add, "But I would feel very much better about it if you and perhaps P.C. Shaw were there, too."

We talked about it some more after that, discussing possible ways and means. After a while, I called Susan to bring us another brandy and soda each; then I called her again and told her just to bring the decanter along with the soda siphon. When she brought them, I invited her to stay and discuss the matter with us. She had a number of intelligent suggestions, and I could see Inspector Harper eyeing her with interest. If it were Scotland Yard policy to employ women as detectives, I suspect he would be trying to hire her away from me.

When he finally left, the hour was far advanced, the brandy decanter was empty, and I had secured at least a provisional agreement to proceed with my plan.

CHAPTER 17

Proceeding on the assumption that "if it were done when 'tis done, then 'twere well it were done quickly," I sat down the next morning and dashed off a note to Mrs. Langley, telling her I was willing to sit for her again.

Return post brought two closely-written pages expressing her joy and gratitude. In our next exchange of letters, we set the date for two days hence, and I was careful to stipulate that both she and her husband would need to be there, exactly as before, in order to ensure the same degree of success. I then wrote notes to Giles Roland and Jim Stern, inviting them to be present likewise. They both accepted, and then there was nothing left to do but prepare the Spirit Parlour for the coming performance.

The most important preparation was to remove the dummy Spiritograph—which had been occupying the parlour ever since the Langley séance—and to replace it once again with the real one. After Susan and I had done this, I stood back and surveyed the room, trying to see it as a first-time observer might. The black velvet curtains hung fantastically looped and festooned and adorned with tassels, fringe, and braided trim. They shut out all light from the bay that overlooked the street. Statues of gods and goddesses loomed dimly in the shadows. The Moroccan lamp hung over the centre of the table, and a Persian rug glowed in tones of black, amber, and gold against the polished floor. The Japanese screen all but concealed the ventilator on the wall to the right of my chair. Susan and I had set five chairs instead of four this time, to accommodate Mr. Stern as well as the three original clients.

"Looks all right," said Susan, surveying the room in her turn. "Everything in order."

"Yes," I agreed. My eye dwelt for a little time on the chair to the right of mine, where Charles Langley would sit. This was the same place he had occupied last time, Dear Reader. I disliked having him so close to me, but putting him anywhere else might warn him that his guilt was already suspected. Besides, if he lashed out at me during the séance, as I rather expected he might, it would be the best possible proof of his guilt. Still, it was not a pleasant prospect.

"You know P.C. Shaw will be behind the screen," said Susan, reading my thoughts. "That's not more than a step away. And the Inspector said you was to duck under the table if Langley showed the least sign of becoming violent. He and Shaw will take over from there."

"Yes," I said again. Since the table was such a large and heavy one, it ought, theoretically, to provide a solid barrier against Langley, assuming I could move quickly enough to take advantage of its protection. But I could not move too quickly, for I had to give him time to make his violent intentions toward me obvious to the witnesses in the room. It was a nice little problem. I went and stood behind Langley's chair, gauging the distance from it to mine and the probable speed with which he could reach me: all too short, and all too swiftly, respectively.

For a moment (and not the first such moment), I wondered why I had ever volunteered to be the tethered goat. Then I reminded myself of Elizabeth Langley and Jenny Taylor. If I did not avenge them, it was quite possible that no one ever would.

"Tonight, we are on the side of Truth and Justice," I told Susan, and she nodded solemnly.

As I spoke the word "Justice," I caught sight of the statue just behind Charles Langley's chair. It was a beautiful little bronze of Themis, one of the household goods of a bankrupt barrister that I had picked up cheaply at auction. Themis, goddess of justice, with her sword and scales and blindfold: what could be more appropriate? As an artist, I take pleasure in these little touches.

"Susan, I'd like to move the statue of Justice so that it will face Charles Langley during the sitting," I said.

Susan thought this notion fanciful and unnecessary. I insisted, however, and in the end I carried my point. She grumbled a bit as we took Themis off her pedestal and swapped her with the statue opposite, a Hindoo goddess of fierce aspect, heavily armed (in every sense) with an impressive array of weaponry. Her plinth was a little too low and wide for Themis to appear to full advantage, but the artistic part of me was satisfied; and after inquiring sarcastically if I wanted also to swap the Persian rug for the coconut matting in the corridor, Susan took herself downstairs while I went up to my bedroom to dress for the séance.

I will not pretend I was not nervous, Dear Reader. I was very nervous indeed as I shadowed my eyes with extra care and draped my head with a lace-edged veil. I usually wear evening dress for séances, meaning trailing skirts, heavy corsetry, and deep décolletage. Tonight, however, I wore a black serge walking dress with a high collar (reinforced once again with carpet tacks), a waist that required only a token amount of corseting, and an ankle-length skirt. It was important that I wear nothing tonight that might hamper my ability to move quickly. The dress's loose flowing sleeves might pose some slight risk in this direction, but I had a particular reason for wanting to keep my arms well hidden. Once I had stepped into my silver-trimmed Turkish slippers (much more conspicuous than usual owing to my abbreviated skirt), I was ready.

When I went downstairs, I found Inspector Harper had arrived in my absence. It was obvious he was even more nervous than I was. Oddly enough, I found this comforting, and some of my own nervousness fell away.

"How you ever talked me into this, I can't imagine," he said grimly.

"Because it's your best hope of getting a conviction against Charles Langley," I said in heartening tones.

"Yes, that's what I told the Chief. And that's the only reason he's allowing me to go through with this business. I may say, however, that he didn't like the idea above half. In fact, not that much. It's my job on the line tonight."

I could have pointed out that I had more than that on the line, but I forbore. He knew it as well as I did, as was clear from his next words.

"Remember, if Langley makes any move against you—*any move at all*—you're to go—"

"Under the table," I said. "I am to go under the table. I know, Inspector Harper: Susan has been reminding me as well."

His eyes dwelt on me unhappily. "I wish I could be sure you would do it, and quickly, too. I don't like seeing a—a lady putting herself at such risk."

I suspected that "lady" was a polite euphemism for "woman of a certain age," but in any case I did not hold it against him. I am certainly not as young as I used to be, but in my youth I was (if I may say so) outstanding for agility. And though my present career no longer demands the ability to free myself swiftly from rope bonds, or to lift a heavy table using only the toes of one foot, I have taken care never to let my physical abilities lapse entirely. There are, as I mentioned early on, fashions in Spiritualism, and one never knows when some of these old fashions may come around again.

To distract the Inspector, I observed that the hour of the séance was drawing near, and that it was time he and the other police officers concealed themselves. There were three of them with us tonight. P.C. Shaw's rôle was purely physical: he was going to be in the Spirit Parlour, behind the Japanese screen, so as to be on hand immediately in case of need. Inspector Harper was going to be in the next room with Susan, watching and listening through the ventilator. With him would be a police stenographer, a colourless-looking man of middle years whom the Inspector introduced as Mr. Norris. Mr. Norris would be taking down the proceedings in shorthand. Both he and the Inspector were slightly taken aback to see how well our working arrangements were adapted to surveillance.

"You have a ventilator *between* these two rooms?" said Mr. Norris, looking at me suspiciously. "Whatever for? It would be much more sensible to have the ventilator in the outside wall, to bring in fresh air."

I said vaguely that it had been a freak of the builder's. In fact, the ventilator had really been my idea, Dear Reader. The workmen I had hired to install it had done so without protest, however, and indeed, they had mentioned putting a similar ventilator between rooms in an old house over in Surrey. I thought the police attitude on this occasion a little excessive. There is no law against ventilators that do not ventilate. One would have supposed I intended to commit some recherché form of murder.[5]

In any case, they had to admit my ventilator was useful on this occasion. With the lights extinguished in their room (save only a low watch-light for Mr. Norris to write by), they would be able to see and hear everything going on in the Spirit Parlour next door. Once Susan had admitted the clients, she was to join them there, and to assist as necessary. With these arrangements made, the stage was set, and it only remained for the rest of the cast to join us.

---

5 The police attitude on this occasion may be explained by the activities of the late Dr. Grimesby Roylott, which took place in 1881-3 but were not publicly revealed until 1892 by famous chronicler of crime Dr. John H. Watson. Full details of the case may be found in "The Adventure of the Speckled Band." Readers unfamiliar with the story would be well advised not to read it before going to bed, or in a room with a suspicious ventilator.—*Ed.*

CHAPTER 18

G iles Roland was the first of the clients to arrive. He did not look happy to be there, and after our initial exchange of greetings, he admitted he was not.

"When I received your invitation, I was minded to decline, but Mrs. Langley asked me to attend as a personal favour," he told me in his cool, precise voice. "Of course I could not refuse her. Indeed, I would be happy if there were some result from tonight's sitting, for the police have been very intrusive—very intrusive indeed. As long as the crime remains unsolved, their persecution—for really, I can call it little else—is likely to continue. And there is no doubt that the result we got last time was very impressive, Madame Fox. I may say that it has made quite a believer of me, as regards Spiritualism. But for all that, I cannot like it. It all left—how can I say it?—a most *disagreeable* impression upon me."

That was not surprising, Dear Reader. Tonight bade fair to be even more disagreeable, but I did not tell him so. I merely offered him a glass of sherry, and left him sipping it with an expression of prim discomfort as I went off to greet the second of the clients, whom Susan had just ushered into the Sitting Room.

This was Jim Stern. I was pleased to see that he was alone. I had been half afraid his sister Cora would accompany him, even without an invitation.

Mr. Stern was looking as bellicose as Giles Roland was prim. "I'm here," he told me. "And I hope to God something comes of it. I tell you, I've had all I can stand from the police. Pardon my language, Madame Fox, but I'd compound with the Devil himself if it was a means of putting an end to this business."

There are those who confound Spiritualism with Satanism, but it is not a comparison I encourage. I frowned and told him that I trusted no such measures would be necessary. Meanwhile, Mr. Roland was gaping at us both, obviously unaware till now that Elizabeth Langley's other suitor was to be present. "You!" he exclaimed. "What are you doing here?"

"I've as good a right to be here as you, Roland," said Mr. Stern, setting his jaw like a bulldog.

"Mr. Stern is interested in seeing Justice done also, Mr. Roland," I said soothingly. "Like you, he has been a victim of police persecution."

Even finding themselves on this common ground did not incline Mr. Roland and Mr. Stern toward friendship. But I gave Mr. Stern his own glass of sherry, topped off Mr. Roland's, and left them eyeing each other with mutual distrust as the doorbell sounded a third time. I knew whom I would be facing now, and I was determined to do it gracefully.

How does one properly greet one's attempted murderer when he visits one in one's home? Etiquette books are strangely silent on the subject. They are equally silent on the subject of how one greets his oblivious wife, whom one hopes to enlighten as to his murderous tendencies in the course of the evening. I think I did it pretty well, Dear Reader. I looked them both in the eye, inclined my head in a gracious nod, and murmured that the evening was a fine one and that the Omens bade fair for a productive sitting.

Mrs. Langley responded by thanking me again for agreeing to sit tonight. But both her voice and manner were more subdued than they had been at our previous meeting. I wondered how much trouble she had had convincing her husband to come. He himself said nothing at all during our exchange of greetings. His eyes met mine once, fleetingly, but after that he stood with his arms folded across his chest, looking down at the floor, up at the ceiling—anywhere but at me and his wife.

He started nervously when I offered him a glass of sherry, but accepted it with a nod of thanks and another fleeting glance. Close up, I noticed there was a smell of alcohol about him already, as though he had had a drink or two beforehand to fortify his courage. I found this distinctly encouraging. As you may know, Dear Reader, drink slows the reactions and dulls the thought processes, and as far as I was concerned, the slower the one and the duller the other, the better.

I also took care to scrutinize him carefully for any sign that he might be carrying a weapon. I could see no such sign: his well-tailored coat, vest, and trousers showed no suspicious bulges, such as a concealed firearm typically produces. This, too, was encouraging. Of course a firearm would be a deplorable weapon to use in a dark room full of people, for much as he might want to kill me, he would be taking a chance of also killing his own wife, or one of his neighbours, or (if he only knew it) a policeman. But I could not depend upon him to see the matter in this sensible light.

"It is time," I announced, when the clients had had as much sherry as they seemed inclined to drink. "Let us begin."

I led the way to the Spirit Parlour and directed everyone to his or her seat. I put the two young gentlemen side by side on my left, with Mrs. Langley across the table from me. Charles Langley, of course, was seated to my right. I hoped he appreciated the view of Themis, but he kept his head down and his eyes fixed on the Spiritograph.

"Let us place our hands on the table," I said.

Mr. Roland, on my left, reached out to take my hand as before. I shook my head at him, however. "No, we need not hold hands this time. Simply place your hands on the table outstretched, so your little fingers just touch your neighbours'."

I had changed my normal procedure, in part to spare Mr. Roland and Mr. Stern from having to hold each other's hands, but mainly because I myself did not want to hold hands with Charles Langley. Even to touch fingers with him was more than I cared to do, and in fact I was wearing gloves that evening so I did not have any actual contact with him at all. Normally I wear mitts rather than gloves, in order to show off my collection of pretty rings, but I was forgoing that little conceit tonight. My only jewelry was the rings on my thumbs, in case I had to operate the Spiritograph using my hands rather than my feet. Wearing rings over gloves is a vulgarity, of course, but there are occasions when we all have to compromise our sense of style.

With the lamps extinguished, the candle in the hanging lamp cast its flickering light over the table and our outstretched hands. I pretended to shut my eyes, but kept them open just enough so that I could watch Charles Langley from beneath my lashes. He sat rigidly in his chair, staring fixedly at the Spiritograph. I could hear his faint rasping breath and see the tendons in his neck standing out.

It is normal Spiritualistic practice to make one's clients wait a bit before the action begins. It should be a long enough wait to sharpen their appetite for the coming phenomena, but not so long that they lose all zest for it. Tonight the issue was complicated by our having a murderer in our midst—and the police as well. In addition to Charles Langley's rasping breath, I could clearly hear P.C. Shaw's stomach rumbling behind the screen. Susan had given him supper in the kitchen according to her usual practice, and now his digestive processes were making themselves heard. I did not think it was obvious to the others, but it seemed to me better not to give them time to notice it. Lifting my head, I raised my voice in a sing-song chant.

"Is there a disembodied spirit in the room?"

A little stir of air made the candle flicker. I mentally applauded Susan for being on cue.

"Is there a disembodied spirit in the room?"

I braced myself as I spoke. Last time there had been that cold earthen smell, but Susan and I had agreed it would not be fitting this time around. Elizabeth Langley was no longer in her grave, after all, but in ashes. And so, as I spoke, the room was immediately filled with the smell of ashes. It was horribly effective. Mrs. Langley uttered a heart-breaking little cry, and I saw Charles Langley give a galvanic start, half rise from his chair, and then settle himself again with an effort.

"Is there a disembodied spirit in the room?" I intoned for the third time. And as I spoke, I pressed my left slipper to the switch.

The silvery chime of the bell produced gasps all around—except from Charles Langley. He merely stared at the Spiritograph with a set jaw.

"Is this the Spirit of Elizabeth Langley?" I asked. The bell rang again, and this time there were sighs around the table. I drew a deep breath.

"Elizabeth Langley, your life on Earth ended in a sad and untimely death," I said, putting all the pathos I could into my voice. "We grieve for you, knowing that your Spirit is not at rest. We meet tonight in hopes of learning more of how you met your death, and to see that Justice is done."

"Yes," said Mrs. Langley, softly.

"Yes," said Mr. Stern, loudly and defiantly.

"Yes," echoed Mr. Roland, a beat behind.

I turned my head and looked full at Charles Langley. He wet his lips, tried to speak, and finally managed to croak out, "Yes."

"Elizabeth Langley," I went on, "we beg you to help us solve the mystery of your death. Why was it necessary for you to die?"

Spellbound, the other four at the table watched the wheel spell out G-U-I-L-T.

"Guilt?" cried Mrs. Langley. "But what guilt, Elizabeth? We don't understand."

This was the critical moment. Slowly, watching Mr. Langley's face all the while, I spelled out B-L-O-O-D.

"Blood," said Mr. Roland blankly.

"Blood?" said Mrs. Langley.

Mr. Langley was looking sick. Again he wet his lips, then glanced around the room like a hunted animal. Again I began to spell.

"B-L-O-O-D," said Mr. Roland, watching the wheel. "Blood . . . on . . . sheets."

There was a long, charged silence. Mrs. Langley looked frozen with horror, her eyes enormous in her fine-boned face. "Elizabeth," I said, lowering my voice until it was hardly more than a whisper. "Who did this? Who hurt you, and then murdered you to hide his guilt?"

I thought Charles Langley was going to break then, but he held on grimly. Slowly and remorselessly the wheel spelled out P-A-P-A. I looked at Mr. Langley. Everyone looked at him. It was Mrs. Langley who finally broke the silence.

"You?" she said, and then, "O God! I see it now. You—and then you killed her."

As she spoke, she got to her feet, staring at him all the while. I won't soon forget the look on her face, Dear Reader. He actually quailed beneath that look. "I didn't want to," he cried.

But of course it isn't natural for a man like Charles Langley to accept blame. Instead, he passes it along. "This is *your* doing," he said, turning upon me in fury. "I should have killed you at the outset."

As he spoke, he seized my wrist—the wrist of the hand nearest him on the table. No doubt he meant to draw me toward him, the better to strangle or strike me. And that is probably what would have happened, except that instead of bringing me to my feet, the hand he grasped simply came off in his.

There were cries of horror around the table. He stood looking stupidly down at the disembodied hand he was holding, then flung it away. I was already disappearing beneath the table. The last things I saw were P.C. Shaw's face rising like a full moon above the Japanese screen, and Charles Langley lunging for the lamp hanging over the table. An instant later, he had wrenched it from its hook, extinguishing the candle, and the room was plunged into darkness.

From that point on, Dear Reader, I could only guess what was happening. There was a wooden rattle followed by a clatter that I diagnosed as Langley's chair hitting the floor, followed by the Japanese screen. Then there was a louder, brazen crash, like the sound of a gong, followed by a heavy thud. And then there was an even heavier thud, accompanied by a sound oddly reminiscent of a butcher cleaving a joint.

In moments of crisis our sense of time becomes, as Hamlet says, out of joint. It was probably less than a minute before the door of the Spirit Parlour opened and I heard Inspector Harper calling authoritatively for the lamps to be relit, but it seemed much longer.

"Remain where you are, please, ladies and gentlemen," he said, as soon as the room was illumined again. "The police are here. We'll soon have matters in hand." His eyes swept the room, and I saw relief on his face as I emerged from beneath the table. He came toward me, reaching out a hand to help me to my feet. "Madame Fox? Are you hurt?"

"Not in the least," I said, brushing off my skirt.

"But—your hand," said Mr. Roland, goggling. "He pulled off your hand!"

"Not *my* hand," I said. Looking around, I spied it on the floor and picked it up to show him. It was a detachable Spirit Hand, not a real one, from the days when we Spiritualists liked to have an extra hand or two to keep on the table while our real ones were busy beneath it. This one was wonderfully lifelike, made of some substance like India-rubber that gave it the look and feel of real flesh. I had paid a pretty penny for it, and when I peeled off the glove to inspect it more closely, I was relieved to see it did not appear to have suffered any injury from Langley's rough treatment.

Inspector Harper, meanwhile, was scanning the room. "Where's Langley?" he demanded.

"I've got him, sir," cried P.C. Shaw, his voice triumphant but slightly muffled. "Caught him trying to get away."

The Inspector strode across the room to where P.C. Shaw was lying atop Charles Langley. He in turn was lying atop the Hindoo goddess statue, which he had knocked off its pedestal. That, I realized, must have been the gong-like noise I had heard.

"Charles Langley, you are under arrest for the murder of your daughter," Inspector Harper told him. "And for assaulting Madame Seraphina Fox. I must warn you that anything you say will be taken down and used in evidence against you."

There was no reply. "Let him up, Shaw," said Inspector Harper, bending over the two prostrate forms (the statue was, technically, supine). "I've got the handcuffs right here. Langley, you might as well get up. We're taking you to the Yard."

Still there was no reply. Charles Langley lay face down atop the statue without moving a muscle. When finally P.C. Shaw and Inspector Harper rolled him over onto his back, we could all see why.

In one of her many hands the goddess was holding a brazen sickle. It was not sharp, but it had a narrow edge, and this edge had been uppermost when the statue fell. Charles Langley had fallen on top of it. That alone would probably have done him no harm, but then P.C. Shaw had leaped on top of him. P.C. Shaw weighed a good eighteen stone[6], Dear Reader, and was moving fast at the time: the equation of mass times velocity is a simple one. The sickle had pierced Langley's heart, and blood flowed sluggishly out of the wound in his chest when they turned him over. He must have died instantly.

---

6 For American readers, a stone is equivalent to 14 pounds: P.C. Shaw thus weighed approximately 252 pounds.—*Ed.*

CHAPTER 19

Sudden death is always a shocking thing, Dear Reader. Of course there were aspects to this death that made it extra shocking. Mr. Stern swore under his breath; Mrs. Langley stood frozen-faced and wide-eyed; Mr. Roland fell to his knees and was noisily sick. I reflected that the rug was going to need replacing anyway.

After a moment of staring horror, Inspector Harper pulled himself together and ordered Mr. Norris to fetch a doctor and to take word to the Police Commissioner of what had happened.

"Sir, I'm sorry, sir," cried P.C. Shaw, his face shiny with remorse and perspiration.

"Not your fault, Shaw," said the Inspector heavily. "It was an accident, of course. Just take these people into another room and start getting their statements."

Mrs. Langley, however, refused to leave the Spirit Parlour while her husband's body remained in it. Inspector Harper begged, bullied, and cajoled to no effect. I finally told him that I would stay with her and keep her out of his men's way, and with that he had to be content. She allowed me to lead her a little aside, and to help her into a chair, but her eyes remained fixed on the body of the late Charles Langley. For the second time in a week, I found myself wishing I were a painter. Jenny Taylor might be my model for Liberty, but Sophronia Langley would have made an effective Clytemnestra.

Finally, the body was removed, and I suggested to Mrs. Langley that we might adjourn to the Sitting Room. "You need tea—or something stronger," I told her. "All this has been a terrible shock."

She nodded and got to her feet. As I tried to lead her quickly past the bloodstained statue and gory rug, she stopped short and said, "Kali."

"I beg your pardon, ma'am?"

"The statue," she said. "Kali. Kali-Ma." And she began to cry.

I thought it an odd moment for a lesson in Hindoo Mythology, but of course she was in a state of shock, poor lady. The tears at least were a good sign, I reckoned. They might bring her some relief. Certainly crying seemed more natural than her former silent immobility.

It was a long night, Dear Reader. I don't know how many pots of tea Susan had to make, but my tea supply was entirely depleted, and the brandy decanter got emptied again as well. We had police coming and going until dawn. Of course the clients—that is to say, the *surviving* clients—had to stay until the police had questioned them. I think it was Mr. Roland and Mr. Stern who drank most of the brandy. I couldn't get Mrs. Langley to take anything stronger than tea. It seemed to help her, however, for after a while she stopped crying and grew more composed. Indeed, I thought her almost unnaturally composed when she was answering the questions the police asked her and describing the horrific events in the Spirit Parlour.

When she was finished, I was in some doubt as to what to do with her. It seemed wrong to send her home by herself, but I doubted she would want to stay at the Temple of Spiritualism any longer than she had to. Fortunately, Jim Stern stepped into the breach, promising to see her home safely and give her into the hands of her maid. Mr. Roland, as usual a beat behind, said Mr. Stern need not trouble himself, and that *he* would take her home. I ruled for Mr. Stern, however.

He had always struck me as the more effectual of the two men, and since his family's property adjoined that of the Langleys, he was the natural choice in any case.

I caught only a glimpse or two of Inspector Harper throughout these events. He was there, but extremely busy. It was another policeman who took down my own statement, and very unsatisfactory he found it, too. I wasn't about to explain how the Spiritograph worked, or tell him how I had learned about such details as the blood on the sheets, so he was left with the impression that I was either an inveterate liar (true, as far as it goes) or in league with the Powers of Darkness (not true, as I devoutly hope).

I had thought perhaps Inspector Harper would come and talk to me before he left, but it was P.C. Shaw, still looking unnaturally pale and shaken, who informed me that the police were finished with their work.

"But I'll stay and guard your premises, ma'am," he said. "Better you and Susan shouldn't answer the door. I'll take care nobody doesn't come inside who hasn't any business to." Quite a little crowd of curiosity-seekers had gathered on the pavement outside, attracted by the coming and going of the police. One or two were newspaper reporters, who had already made various ingenious efforts to get inside.

"And the Inspector?"

"He had to leave, ma'am, but he said to tell you he'd wait on you later." And with that I had to be content.

"Later" turned out to be almost a week later. In the interim, the crowds outside dwindled, until at last we were troubled by nothing more than an occasional pedestrian dawdling along and gawking up at the sign that read "Temple of Spiritualism."

In reading the newspaper accounts, I was relieved to see the affair had been largely hushed up. No doubt this was in deference to Mrs.

Langley's feelings. Charles Langley was stated to have been guilty of his daughter's death by his own confession, and to have been fatally injured in the course of his arrest. The more lurid aspects of the story were rigidly suppressed. My own rôle was not mentioned at all, although my place of business was. I was resigned to that, however, and felt that it could have been much worse.

Six days after the death of Charles Langley, late in the afternoon of a dark and dreary day, Susan announced that the Inspector was there to see me. I took my time getting ready, then came down to the Sitting Room in full Spiritualistic regalia. It might well be my last appearance as such—although I had thought that last time, too. I was reminded of an operatic prima donna, giving a series of positively last farewell performances.

The Inspector rose to his feet as I came in, disentangling his long legs from among the clutter of little tables, ottomans, and what-nots with which my Sitting Room is furnished. I gave him my hand, and he retained it a moment, looking down at me.

"Good afternoon, Madame Fox," he said.

"Good afternoon, Inspector Harper," I said. "Please be seated. Would you like some tea?"

He said that he would, and I rang the bell for Susan. Once she had brought the tea-tray, I told her I wouldn't need her any more that day, and that she might take the afternoon off. She threw a doubtful look at me, another at the Inspector, and finally withdrew with an air of going against her better judgment.

I poured the tea, handed the Inspector his cup, and settled back in my chair.

"You have probably seen the accounts in the newspapers," he said. "Of course we kept the matter as quiet as we could, for Mrs. Langley's sake. But I thought I would come in person to give you the full details, and to wrap up the loose ends, as it were."

I nodded, wondering what he meant by loose ends. My imagination had already conjured up images of thread, with my livelihood hanging thereby. Aloud, I said, "I have been curious to learn how the Police Commissioner reacted when he heard about Langley's death. I know you said he was dubious about the idea of getting a confession in the first place. What did he say about the way the case turned out?"

The Inspector laughed, rather ruefully. "Well, it's certain I won't be making promotion over it," he said. "But between you and me, I'm inclined to think now it might have been for the best. It would have been a hellish business to prosecute. The Chief acknowledged it and agreed that Langley's death, unfortunate as it was, might have saved a lot of trouble all around."

"Indeed," I said, "and not least for poor Mrs. Langley. I was glad for her sake the matter never came to trial."

"No doubt, no doubt," agreed the Inspector. "But it was a bad business nonetheless. Poor Shaw feels it, as you might expect."

"No one could blame him for what happened," I protested. "It was so clearly an accident."

"Yes, but it might have been avoided, if he'd followed orders." The Inspector, looking exasperated, ran his hand through his hair. "He lost his head entirely when the lights went out. And we had prepared for that very eventuality! He had a dark lantern, and he was supposed to slide it open before he did anything else. But he was so excited, he just went for Langley in the dark—and of course you know what happened after that."

"But would it have made any difference?" I asked. "Opening the lantern would only have taken a second. He would probably still have caught Langley on top of the statue."

The Inspector acknowledged that this was likely. "About that statue," he went on, regarding me with his sternest expression. "Once everything was over, a couple of my men took it upon themselves to clean it up a bit and put it back on its pedestal. And they said the pedestal was really too small for such a big, heavy thing. They said it wasn't any wonder it got knocked over."

Waving an airy hand, I said I was planning to put it on a different pedestal anyway. "In any case, it wasn't P.C. Shaw's fault, and you may tell him I said so. In fact, I think he ought to get a medal for putting Langley down."

"Between you and me, I agree. But you can't expect Shaw himself to feel the same way. Poor chap, he signed up to apprehend criminals, not to execute them. And he's really a sensitive fellow at bottom, though you mightn't think it to look at him."

"Well, tell him he may come around to the Temple of Spiritualism any time he chooses, and Susan and I will try to make him feel better."

The Inspector promised to pass the message along. "I am glad to hear you have changed your attitude about the police," he said, looking at me very seriously. "That was another thing I wanted to talk to you about. You were a great help over this case. In fact, there wouldn't have *been* a case, if it weren't for you. Even if things didn't turn out quite the way I would have liked, I wanted to thank you for your help."

I said he was quite welcome. There was a pause. "It was a great relief to me that you came to no harm the other night," he went on. "Langley was a dangerous man, and there's no doubt he meant to do you an injury." He eyed me carefully. "That extra hand of yours gave me quite a turn. Would you mind showing me how you did that?"

It is always flattering to have one's cleverness admired, Dear Reader. I fetched the Spirit Hand, and showed him how, if you were wearing wide, flowing sleeves, you could easily conceal it until the time came to sit at the table. "You hold it in your real hand, so, with your elbow bent—and it protrudes from your sleeve and looks like your real hand. The more so because I was wearing gloves that night. I put one glove on my left hand, and the other on the Spirit Hand, and no one could have told them apart. Then when I sat at the table, I simply laid the Spirit Hand on the edge of the table, with the sleeve covering it to the wrist. My real hand was entirely free, beneath the table."

"Beneath the table," he repeated. "I wondered about that, too. I suppose that's how you manage your Spiritualistic tricks?"

I simply smiled and shook my head. Of course he was on a false trail, Dear Reader, but I saw no need to set him right. You cannot expect a Fox to give a hound a straightforward run. In any case, he surprised me by saying that my secrets were safe with him.

"I told you at the outset that there was no reason why the police should interfere with your business. And I'm a man of my word. In fact," he said, drawing a deep breath, "in fact, I wondered if you might consider giving us a hand now and then in other matters? As I said before, you're in a position to see and hear a lot of things we aren't. You might tip us the wink if you hear of anything we ought to know."

I told him I would think about it. Of course it would put me in a delicate position, mediating between him on one side and Felicity and her compatriots on the other. But mediation is, after all, what a Medium does, Dear Reader. And I like to think no one does it better than I do.

His next comment surprised me, too. "In truth, you'd be doing me a favour if you'd just allow me to come by now and then and talk to you. I found it very helpful to get a woman's perspective on this case. And there aren't many women one could talk to about a case like this." A kind of sadness overspread his face. "My wife—she could never bear to hear about something as ugly as this business, much less talk about it."

"Your wife?" I repeated. I was greatly surprised to hear he was married, Dear Reader. I do not mean that he had shown any tendency to fondle my hand, like Mr. Waggoner—that is not a reliable indicator in any case. But I consider myself an observant woman, and I had observed none of the obvious stigmata of the married man in his appearance.

"My late wife," he said, making matters clear. "She died a few years ago."

"I am very sorry to hear of your loss," I said formally.

He shook his head, clearly not wishing to dwell on the subject. I thought I could read between the lines. Really happy marriages, with both parties equal in affection and united in interest, are rare in this world. Human Nature being what it is, one is safe in assuming that any given union leaves something, somewhere, to be desired.

He did not exactly admit this, but said again that his late wife could not bear to hear about the uglier aspects of police work. "And of course the hours were a trial to her." He looked at me rather speculatively. "I suppose, working nights yourself, you would understand the difficulty."

I agreed that I might, and another brief silence ensued. The Inspector broke it by taking a yellowed theatre bill out of his pocket. "I ran across this, a few weeks ago," he said. "I thought it might interest you."

The headline act of the bill was a young American Medium, Mary Marion, whose powers were vaunted in glowing terms and who was described as making her first European tour. It was dated some decades back. "This Mary Marion," he said, watching me as I read it. "Had you ever heard of her?"

"No," I said firmly, folding the bill and returning it to him.

"She sounds like an interesting character," he said. "I did a bit of investigating into her background. She was American-born, but had an English mother. The mother was rather an exceptional lady by the sound of it: daughter of an Oxford don, and very learned and clever in her own right."

"Ah," I said, with polite disinterest.

"She seems not to have been so clever about men and marriage, however. Against her parents' wishes, she eloped with a fellow named Marion—an American, he was. It wasn't a bad match, on the face of it. He came from a good old Southern family, with a war hero or two in the background and all that sort of thing."

"Yes?" I said, still looking politely disinterested.

"Still, it wasn't a very happy marriage, as things turned out. It seems Marion was rather a ne'er-do-well, and their affairs went steadily downhill in spite of everything his wife could do. She ended up dying when their only child was still pretty young. That was this girl, Mary," he said, tapping the theatre bill. "And then when the Spiritualism business sprang up over in the States, and it was clear there was money to be made out of it, it sounds as if her father thought he could get rich promoting his daughter as a Medium."

"There were many of us who began in the business around that time," I said in a non-committal voice.

"But you never heard of this Mary Marion?"

"Certainly not," I said with decision. "I can't imagine why you think I would have."

"Because I thought she looked a bit like you." The Inspector held out the theatre bill again to show me. "There's her picture, see? Quite a beautiful girl."

"I was never beautiful," I said, firmly and accurately.

"Ah, you're too modest," he said, shooting me a sidelong smile.

Even if he is a policeman, Dear Reader, I feel I may have to cultivate his acquaintance. I have occasionally been called beautiful in the course of my lifetime, but he is the only man who has ever called me modest.

CHAPTER 20

Naturally, I lost no time acquainting Susan with the substance of my conversation with Inspector Harper. She was very relieved to learn there was no immediate need for us to leave London.

"The Inspector wouldn't be talking about your helping the police if he meant to shut you down as a fraud," she said shrewdly.

"No, and thanks to the Spirit Hand business, he would be on the wrong track even if he did." I laughed aloud at the thought. "If you're going to grasp the nettle, that is certainly the kind of hand to use!"

It was a comfort to have the secret of the Spiritograph still secret to everyone but us, Dear Reader. For it appears likely I will be using it again. I had feared that the Langley business might put off my clientele, but in fact the opposite seems to be true. Just enough of the facts have filtered out to hint at a mystery, and there is something about mystery that people—even well-born English people—find irresistible. The Gilberts, Lady Haverhill, and my other regular clients have all been clamouring for me to sit for them again. Susan and I have put the Spirit Parlour in order, and it is ready for business whenever I decide that I am ready, too.

You may be thinking that in putting my parlour in order, I would have got rid of the statue of Kali. But you would be wrong,

Dear Reader. I am not a soft-hearted woman, and the idea that a vicious murderer met his end through its agency only enhances its value in my eyes. Susan and I put Kali back on her proper plinth, and there she remains, waving her weaponry and glaring her fearful grimace.

"I can't imagine the Hindoos worshipping such a thing," Susan told me in confidence. She was a little nervous speaking in front of the statue itself, and I couldn't altogether blame her. "Frighten a body to death, I should think. What's she a goddess of?"

"That's a curious thing," I said. "I have done some research on the subject since the other night. It seems that among other things she's a goddess of death and destruction, which certainly fits her appearance. But in at least some parts of India, she's also worshiped as a mother goddess—a loving mother, believe it or not. Kali-Ma: Mother Kali."

"That's . . . interesting," said Susan.

"It is, isn't it?" I said.

I thought of Mrs. Langley a great deal in the days that followed. Under the circumstances, however, I never expected to hear from her again. It was therefore a great surprise to receive a letter from her, only a few days after the Inspector's visit, tying up yet another loose thread.

She began by saying that recent events had made England unbearable to her. That was a conclusion I could hardly wonder at. In consequence, she had decided to sell the Arbours and return to India. She wrote that she had warm friends in the Anglo-Indian community there who would take her in, and that she also had some idea of looking up Reema, her daughter's ayah, whom she thought of taking to live with her as a companion:

Reema and I both loved Elizabeth, and it will be a comfort to be with someone else who will mourn my daughter along with me. At the same time, I do not forget what you told me about the danger of keeping my eyes fixed on the past. The future seems to hold little enough promise at present, but I am willing to believe hope and even happiness might lie there nonetheless.

Thank you again for all you have done, Madame Fox. Please believe I will never regret that you gave me the truth; only that I was too blind not to recognize it sooner.

Enclosed with this letter was a cheque that made me blink. Mrs. Langley had been as good as her word, and it was the reward money doubled, as she had promised. Susan heard my exclamation and came over to see what the matter was.

I held the cheque out to her mutely. She looked at it and whistled. "It's an ill wind," she said.

"Don't," I said. "That poor woman! It makes me sick to think what I brought upon her, and here she is thanking me for it."

"That's not very logical," said Susan at once. "You didn't bring anything upon her. You just uncovered what was already there. And gracious knows what would have happened if you hadn't. Her husband would have gone on in his nasty ways, and maybe he'd have murdered her, too, one of these days."

That made me feel a little better, Dear Reader. But I still could not help grimacing as I shoved the cheque into the Receivables pigeonhole of my writing desk. "You're not going to be fool enough to refuse it, are you?" demanded Susan, wide-eyed.

"No," I said. "But I cannot help wishing I had earned it differently. Or even that I had not earned it at all, if only I could have restored her daughter to her unharmed."

Susan studied me a moment with an odd smile on her face. "Well, that just shows you've got a soul above money," she said. "Who would have thought it?"

⚮

Who indeed, Dear Reader? But in a way, it is rather a comfort. As is the money, of course. High-minded people might think I ought to refuse money earned in such a way, but I have never claimed to be high-minded. And indeed, those who speak loftily about refusing money have never been stranded in a provincial town, literally without a penny or any means to earn one, because one's husband absconded with one's accumulated earnings and all the paraphernalia of one's trade.

Technically, of course, he was not really my husband. But at the time he was fulfilling the duties associated with that rôle, including, unfortunately, being custodian of our joint funds. That's another reason I have never married. Susan points out, however, that the recent passage of the Married Women's Property Act has eased some of the disadvantages of the married state.

"And you said the Inspector's a widower," she added slyly. "Everybody knows widowers are easy prey. A clever woman like you, I've no doubt you could catch him if you wanted to."

"Nonsense," I said at once. "He's a policeman, for heaven's sake. Whatever put such an idea in your head?"

"It's been there for a while. Policeman or not, it's easy to see he admires you."

"I daresay," I said shortly. "He doesn't know me." I thought about that for a while, then amended, "He doesn't know *everything* about me. And besides," I added, as she opened her mouth to argue, "my heart will always belong to P.C. Shaw."

⁓

So that is how I earned the first honest money of my life, Dear Reader, as well as becoming hand-in-glove with a police detective. I have not yet decided what to do with my little fortune. Properly invested, it will be a useful hedge against old age and infirmity, and I will doubtless devote most of it to that purpose. But I plan to spend part of it, too. I have, after all, been at some expense about this business. Not only did the rug in the Spirit Parlour need to be replaced, but I later discovered that P.C. Shaw had put his foot through the Japanese screen.

I think, too, of expanding my establishment. Jenny Taylor came to call the other day, using another of her precious half-days so that she might thank me for what she graphically called "putting an end to that filthy bastard." (Again, I apologize for the vulgarity, Dear Reader.) It was clear she could not decide whether I had brought about his death via Occult Agency, or simply by way of my underworld connections (clearly she has taken Felicity's measure). But in any case, she is disposed to regard me as a heroine.

It struck me that I might do well to hire her away from her current employer. At present I have a couple of daily women who come in to do my heavy cleaning, but though this arrangement has been satisfactory in the main, I find such women require close supervision. Susan has really enough to do, considering she not only cooks but helps me with the Spiritualism business.

If Jenny were to join us, she could take over as housekeeper and leave Susan free for the other work. I have talked the matter over with Susan, and she is in favour of the plan—of course, it would mean a promotion for her as well as for Jenny. Given the nature of my business, I do not like to have servants living-in whom I cannot wholly trust, but I think I *can* trust Jenny. We are united by a bond that goes deeper than the usual employee-employer relationship.

It pleases me to think I can help her to an easier life, after all she has suffered. There is a surprising pleasure in this business of doing good, I find. Still, you must not be thinking that I am *entirely* a reformed character, Dear Reader. The leopard does not change his spots, or the Fox her devious ways. I have worked hard to build up my clientele, and I don't propose to abandon it—especially since most of my clients are so feckless that they would simply fall into the hands of someone far less principled than I am.

What is more, I have been thinking over the Inspector's proposition, and I believe I see my way clear to taking on a certain amount of the kind of work lawyers call *pro bono publico:* for the public good. One of my retired colonels came around the other day to consult the Spirits about an investment in an American gold mine. Looking at the prospectus, I instantly recognized the handiwork of one of my partners-in-crime from years ago. I think the Spirits will warn my colonel against that particular investment, Dear Reader. A good shepherdess lets no one shear her sheep but herself.

This, then, concludes my account of my one and only brush with genuine Occult Phenomena. I am still uncertain how much credit for those phenomena is due to me, if indeed any of it is. Susan points out that it was all my doing, in a sense. It was I who invented the Spiritograph; I who was so antagonized by Charles Langley's manner that I elected to sit for his wife even against my better judgment; I who made the fateful decision to swap the statues in the Spirit Parlour. So perhaps I do have psychic powers heretofore unsuspected—or, as Susan so graciously puts it, perhaps I am "not a complete fraud."

It may be so, Dear Reader. There is a part of me that would like to believe it, but in fact all these actions are explainable by ordinary means. I have been a skeptic so long that I am loath to abandon my skepticism at this late date. So I have been doing some reading on the subject, trying to find an explanation that lies in the natural rather than supernatural realm.

There are authorities who argue that such techniques as Spirit Writing and Trance Speaking are not ways of communing with Spirits at all, but rather with the Medium's own subconscious mind. In that case, it may not have been I, but rather Sophronia Langley with her burning desire to know the truth, who produced the phenomena we witnessed. Or possibly Charles Langley's own guilt found tangible expression at the séance table, proving the old adage that murder will out. Yet though this might explain the movement of a pencil in a planchette, it does not explain how an electrical circuit could have been bypassed through no apparent human action.

Perhaps there is more in Spirit Energy than I supposed.

I have endeavoured to make this account as truthful as I can, Dear Reader, yet there is no denying that in many ways it was an ugly affair—sufficient refutation of Mr. Keats's assertion that Beauty is Truth, and Truth Beauty. Mind you, I know what he means, or think I do (there is no saying with poets, after all). But just as beauty thrills the soul, so the mind thrills to see truth stand clear, undimmed by falsehood and misdirection. Or, to put it another way, there is a pleasure in shining a light in dark places—even when one's natural milieu is the dark.

The End

ABOUT THE AUTHOR

Joy Reed is a reclusive bibliophile and compulsive tea-drinker. Her devotion to the written word is such that she is largely able to block out the clamorings of the modern world, although she does take an occasional peek outside just to make sure the Nihilists haven't totally gotten the upper hand. She collects uranium glass, old etiquette books, big hairy spiders, and far too many other things, despite a recent attempt to change her life through the magic of tidying up. She is the author of sixteen romance novels, an award-winning master's thesis, and the Seraphina Fox mystery series.

You can read her musings about life and literature on her blog BookJoy: http://bookjoy.livejournal.com/

www.ingramcontent.com/pod-product-compliance
Lightning Source LLC
Chambersburg PA
CBHW031331170626
46807CB00002B/643

* 9 780692 768617 *